NEVER BE TOLD

NEVER BE TOLD

Brad Shprintz

Bradley Shprintz

Contents

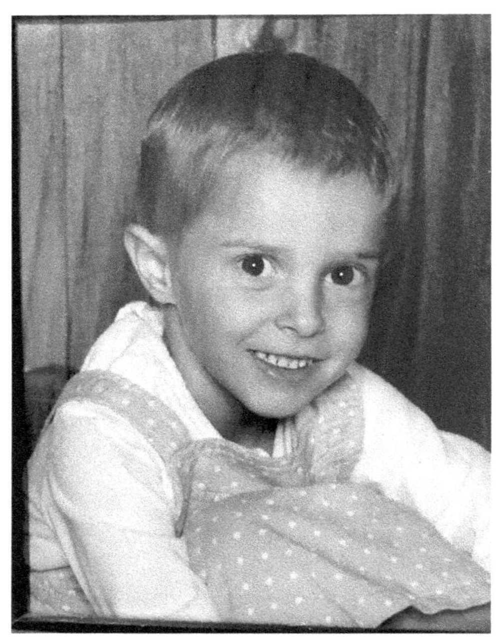

Jayne Alexis Keys
5/1/2008 - 12/8/2012

NEVER BE TOLD is dedicated to Jayne!
Her time here was short yet her impact to all who were
blessed to be around her was wonderful! I was honored to have
known her.

PART 1

1

CAPTAIN JONES

Surreal was the thought Bubba Jones was thinking as he sat in the captain's chair of the starship he was commanding. Just two weeks ago, he was on Earth checking his investments and enjoying life. Decisions made affected nothing more than future profits and what he would eat. Now everything was different. His decisions might cost people their lives.

He felt like he was not ready to do this. If only his best friend were with him to help guide him on his first mission. This was not just his first mission; he was also in command.

Brand Wright was Bubba's best friend. He practically died fighting General Max and was currently in a time capsule suspended from the moment of death by seconds. Bubba was now heading to Earth to retrieve what he has called the "secret cure."

Bubba's mind went back to when Brand had mentioned the rules on how to store and use the Jinn. It was acquired on one of their previous adventures.

In his mind, Brand said, "There are rules that must be followed for the Jinn not to ruin what is wished. First and most importantly, never wish for something dead to come back to life. Your wish must be noble, something that does not benefit you. I know it sounds crazy to have the ability to make a wish and not be able to personally gain from it.

Also, it is just as important who will gain access to the Jinn after you. That type of power must be guarded and given only to someone who will use it wisely."

Bubba realized at the time that it was a special gift but never really comprehended how highly regarded Brand thought of him. He clearly remembers how Brand talked about hiding it until the time it would be needed.

"Now it must be stored in a place where whether there is fire or water, it will not be damaged or found. A place hidden to all eyes yet readily accessible when needed." That was how Brand had phrased it.

Bubba remembered when he tried to tell Brand his idea. Before he could get two words out, Brand stopped him, saying, "No, don't tell me anything. It is strictly on a need to know, and I don't qualify."

Also, when Bubba questioned Brand on where he had hidden it before he bestowed it to him, he finally told him, with a lot of prodding.

"Now Bubba, you got to understand that I did not have very much time, plus I knew it could not be stored at or near my rig."

Bubba remembers how he kept pushing him along. "I hear ya. So, where did you put it?"

"It was only temporary cause I knew you would get it soon. I went to the woods and hid it in the hollow of a dead tree."

Bubba's memories now interpreted all those words and actions differently. Brand was always lucky, and even though he had good advice, he mostly never followed it. That worked for Brand by faking and winging it until the mission was completed.

Bubba Jones understood that for his mission to be successful, he would have to do it his own way. Of course, he would use the advice from his association with Brand to help shape his own decisions. Bubba's instinct was to approach things with more care and planning. He had hidden the treasure in a much more secure and secret place, and that was how he would handle the mission at hand.

———

Bubba's home started as an old farmhouse on 40 acres. A completely new addition was added that became the new home of Bubba Jones.

The farmhouse he turned into a guest home, adding additions both to the farmhouse and the new home attached to it. By the time he finished, the basic contours of the home could not readily be determined.

That fact, and because Bubba was very good with his hands regarding construction, allowed him to add a secret room off his study.

Bubba was very proud of his library study, which had high walls lined with bookshelves from floor to ceiling. Certain people appreciate the value of books. Terms like book lovers don't really do them justice. Like fine wine connoisseurs, they go to a much deeper level of love for their cherished possessions. Of course, there is the construction and age of the book, yet some hold knowledge that is still vaguely known to the modern world.

Then, the way that information is processed by the reader is examined. Between imagination and words, stories that feel more real than reality are formed. Bubba was a book lover, and all those types of people like to hoard their treasure.

On one of the shelves near the top, there was a book that Brand had written called "SUBJECT 9." That book had a wire with a spring trigger that, when tilted out, unlocked that section of bookshelves. It would open by turning in its center, allowing a two-foot passage to the room behind it.

The hidden room looked very similar to the prior room, with only one wall full of books. In the center of the room was a large plush chair with a table in front and a pole lamp hanging over the chair. The short walls had a closet on one side and one large picture on the other.

To most, that would be good enough. Having a secret room that no one was aware of. A place to hide from the world that is cozy and filled with what the owner loves. Yet Bubba Jones was not like most people. Not only was he a self-made multi-millionaire, but he also retained the best parts of himself, being a kind person who never let his ego get in his way. He had a strong liking for esoteric things and was quickly drawn to Brand, who seemed surrounded by the strangest of events.

Near the end of the bookshelves, within the closet, was another secret room. That room was accessed with a magnetic lock that was placed on a certain spot on the closet's back wall. Then, the entire back wall of the closet would open when activated.

That room was small with just a big, very heavy, fireproof safe. The room was built around the safe. It looked like it weighed over 500 pounds and was never leaving its tomb. The safe had an analog-style circular dial that, if turned correctly from right to left to right, would reveal its contents once the large handle was turned.

The crystal skull was covered with back linen that totally enclosed it.

Bubba's thoughts were brought back to his current situation with his two crew members arguing with each other.

Utago, whom he met on Mars, had first tried to kill Brand. After that and other things, he became Brand's biggest fan. Utago prided himself on his bravery. His goal was to become well-known in the galaxy for his strength and fearlessness. He was 8 feet tall with a wide body, and with three fingers plus a thumb on each hand.

He was very similar to an Earth-man but bigger, smarter, and faster. While also being very idealistic. He spoke short, broken English phrases which made his thoughts known.

Jayne was human yet had never been on Earth. That really was not unusual, for there were many species that had wandered into space, having offspring, and never seeing their parents' home worlds.

She was born on the Nevermore, a starship, and raised as a soldier. She had delicate features that hid the opposite, which was her inner strength that shined like a strong aura over her being. She was some-one who was beautiful but never used that beauty to her advantage. She was a walking contradiction wrapped in intensity and mystery. In Earth years, she was 45, yet traveling through space at high speeds gave her a younger appearance.

Jayne had strong opinions on many subjects, with many other topics not caring at all. There was no question about how tough she was. With Utago looming over her, she showed no fear and, at times, shouted many insults directly at him.

Jayne had a short, cropped hairstyle with natural blonde colors. Her body was lean and muscular, and she always moved with high energy.

Regarding her emotions, she did not hide them, regardless of whether they were favorable or not to the issue at hand.

Bubba was a big man, well over 6 feet tall and built big. He had some extra weight, yet it always seemed to be an advantage for him. His hair was a light brown, and his face had large cheeks with a smile that seemed to be shown a lot.

Right now, Utago was arguing with Jayne about how many jumps or folding of space would be needed to get back to Earth. Jayne said it could be done with one, and Utago said two would be better.

The truth was that Bubba did not know which option was best. It was his decision on the issue. Whichever side he chose, the other member who lost would be upset, even if they didn't show it.

Bubba's nature was to try not to hurt people, so the decision was harder than it should have been.

Jayne said it would be faster, and we would just cruise longer in space to get there. Utago's position was that it was bad for the engines and, in the end, would save very little time when the cruising was added.

Now, both were looking at Bubba for his command on what to do.

————

Sam Smith was more powerful than the President of the United States. His title was Senior Advisor to the President, yet, in reality, he knew about and controlled more power than any person on the planet. His nature was to be private and powerful. He would never admit it, but he missed his last personal assistant, Nina Woodhall, who was now Senator Woodhall of Florida. Sam made that happen, which was not hard for him.

His new top person was Pierce, a very contained man who reminded Sam a lot of himself. Pierce was in his mid-thirties and hardly ever changed his facial expressions. Whatever orders Sam pronounced, Pierce did with a poker face. Only speaking with as few words as needed to complete a point or to ask something.

The real question with Pierce was, what was going on inside his head? What did he think about with all that he observed? This feature bothered many around him except for Sam Smith.

If Sam had told him to turn the electricity off in New York, all that Pierce would have said would have been, "Yes, sir. How long would you like it turned off?" Pierce seemed to understand how to do everything when it came to making the government work in the direction of what was needed to complete Sam's commands.

The dark project's industry liked his cold emotionless approach, and he became Sam's liaison with them. Unlike Nina, his predecessor, he seemed to have no other areas of desire except for exactly what he was doing currently.

For a person like Sam Smith, he was perfect. Yet the question of what Pierce thought about was unknown to all.

Sam was sitting behind his big old desk when Pierce knocked on his door.

"Yes, come in."

Pierce walked in and said nothing.

Then Sam said, "I want Bubba Jones' house monitored and, when he returns, him to be detained."

Pierce responded with, "Yes, sir."

Then, as an afterthought, Sam barked out, "Also, have Colonel Bolt in my office at 900 hours tomorrow."

Pierce nodded his head in understanding and left the room.

————

The starship that Bubba was commanding was beautiful and had all the latest features for that type of craft. There were so many neat features that he had never experienced.

One that stood out was what he called the human dishwasher. It had a tube-like structure that was completely sealed once inside it. The circumference of the inside was about 4 feet wide and with a length of 8 feet long. A lounge-type chair was inside, which the person would lie on.

After pushing a few buttons, the fun began. The first thing that you realized was the machine knew exactly where your head and eyes were. The bench started to provide a message as the heated water was spraying you from all sides. Next came a soapy waterfall of water from the top. After that, you were resprayed with fresh, clean water while getting a massage from the bench. From there, it provided a 5-minute wet steam with a splash after that of cold water. If that was not enough, then it heated up and dried the entire body with a blow dry mechanism, similar to a hair dryer, from start to finish in under 15 minutes.

Another aspect that was different from that on Earth was what Bubba called reverse VR. Instead of wearing a headset and seeing the world through it while it added other elements within your view, the reverse happened.

The ship had equipment attached to the ceilings that projected 3D objects in the room, making individual special hardware not needed. When Bubba initiated the room controls, a panel appeared 4 inches from his hand. It could detect his fingers so he could control the switches and dials it projected. Lights, temperature, plus other controls were available while using it. Watching TV or listening to music would appear in the room and could be adjusted to any size or location. Once done, they would just disappear.

Each control would have more options, and you could adjust the lighting as if it were outside with clouds moving overhead. Or set the breeze controls for intermittent gusts at temperatures different from those in the room.

The ship was loaded with devices that provided the same functions you would get on Earth, just so much more advanced.

Bubba, looking at Jayne, said, "This time, we will go with Utago's plan." It was said gently with a little upturn of the lips, trying to form a small smile.

Jayne, who was tired of trying to win her argument, just looked at Utago and said, "Stupid." Then, turning her back to Bubba, she stormed out of the room.

Utago looked at Bubba with a big smile and said, "Women."

Bubba now wondered if he should just have let her have her way, being sure Utago would have taken it better.

Even though either way would hopefully not really matter, these decisions were so much more difficult than just making money.

2

THEY HAVE ARRIVED

Colonel Bolt was sitting in Sam Smith's impressive office, which screamed power. Everything shouted it, from the very large, old, strong wooden desk to each picture on the wall. There were also weapons of war, from an African spear to a prototype of a new weapon and such things.

Both men were very similar in that they were dedicated to their work with no wives or children. Both keepers of many secrets that others would not believe if they even heard them. They were both in their late sixties and with Subject 9, aka Brand Wright, their lifelines were brought together. Yet there was more than that. There was what is really needed for a truly positive relationship, respect for each other.

Colonel Bolt was in charge of many different programs, with one of them being the RB program. Reality Benders are where people can modify physics, plus more, within our current shared realities. Basically, they bend reality in ways that are not supposed to happen. This ability can be scientifically studied without understanding what causes it.

Sam began with, "I want three replacements for Subject 9. Also, how would you like to have my spot? I am planning a trip and my replacement." There was a long pause before Bolt responded.

"Sam, you and Subject 9 can't be replaced. You are both unique, a gestalt that can't be replicated. Subject 9 had just the right traits, plus his

RB abilities, to be extremely effective in getting positive results. It still is hard to determine how much was due to his RB powers compared to his natural abilities in the field. And anyone who replaces you might last a few months to years. You have handled it for decades!"

Now, the silence was on Sam's end. Then, with a smile, which Sam rarely did, he said, "Thanks. We will all be replaced. Provide me with two subjects that we will put into the field with easy assignments to tune them up. Think about my offer."

It was clear that their meeting was over, and Bolt should have started to depart, but he had something more he wanted to discuss. Even though they were friends, Sam was always the boss.

Bolt started with, "Have you ever had a gut feeling about something? I have had them many times and have found them useful. I have no evidence to support anything I say, but I will say it anyhow. I have a bad feeling about Pierce. A feeling he cannot be trusted, that he is not who he seems. I just wanted you to know."

Sam did not respond at all. He just shook his head up and down, acknowledging what was said. Unlike Nina Woodhall, his last assistant, who everyone liked, Pierce had the opposite effect on most people, including Colonel Bolt.

Sam Smith was deep in thought, his mind going into the past to the last time he was with Brand Wright. How powerful that man seemed when, in reality, he had no power at all. How Brand had put himself in danger for really no gain to himself. Sam or Dragonfly could have easily killed him by design or accident, yet Brand had no fear.

For that matter, when Brand fought General Max, and he was now suspended in time, with his last seconds waiting for his death. He just seemed to have no fear, no fear of death. Those short few minutes he was with him had changed Sam. It was the reason Sam was taking the journey to the planet LaTaFree.

Even though Sam knew that Brand was technically still alive, it felt like he had died. And in that death, had become larger than he was in life. Going to the actual place where he had last stood was on Sam's mind.

Now, if anyone really knew him, this would make absolutely no sense. Sam Smith was not a man to follow in anyone's footsteps. That was the strange thing. Brand's imminent death seemed to have changed him.

The mind is a strange place, even to one who controls it. There are things that are not understood and may be better left that way.

Then his thoughts went to Pierce, and seeds of doubt started to emerge. He also felt something else going on in Pierce's head. Yet, when someone is very useful and always available to do whatever is asked, it can lead to letting one's guard down.

There had been so many over the years, and each had fallen when attacking Sam Smith. It is easy to become overconfident when you have decades of control reassuring you of your dominance.

————

Both Jayne and Utago knew how to fly the starship, making Bubba feel a bit inadequate. Yet, without his leadership, no goals would be attained. Knowledge is always important, but also is getting along with each other. Bubba was the glue that held their team together. Without it ever having to be spoken, it appeared everyone accepted his ultimate importance in achieving their quest.

More than that, Bubba had a quiet knowledge about many things. Not one to brag or flaunt his wealth or thoughts, he spoke without words to his crew that he belonged as their captain.

Utago set the controls with Jayne closely watching him, as she definitely did not trust him. It was decided that Bubba and Jayne would take the small shuttle to Bubba's home while Utago monitored them from the starship. In the event they were seen, it would not bring attention to them as they were both human.

Bubba's thoughts went to how far he had come from landing on Mars and becoming overwhelmed with all the different life forms he encountered. In hindsight, they did not try to eat or shoot each other just because they were different. After a little while, he was as fine with them as they were with him.

His thoughts went to how Earth's population was still not ready. That if they saw Utago, given his size and looks, they would shoot first and never ask questions, thinking that shooting Utago would make them a hero.

On the planet LaTaFree, there were so many different beings, all in peace with each other. Earth's people have a long way to go before they can join the Galactic Community. Soon, they were finishing the first space fold with a five-hour delay before their next fold.

Bubba's thoughts were deeply on the mission and what Brand had told him about his past missions. Brand was a good man, yet double-crossing someone was his signature move. Bubba asked him why he would do that, and his answer was as follows.

"Bubba, first you must assume that it will be done to you, so the trick is to do it first, but the timing has to be just right. If done too early, it will be realized, and they will make plans to defeat you. If done too late, it will not matter as they will already have defeated you. Like everything in life, timing is everything!"

Then Bubba's thoughts went to a pregnant woman, which made him smile. Even with the ankle pains, stomach problems, heat issues, mood swings, plus cravings, that is the easy stage. As soon as the baby is born, the hard part begins.

Right now, he was on the easy stage. Once he obtained the Jinn, assuming it was still in its hiding place, the hard part would begin. Then people would be attacking him for that prize.

His thoughts started to develop a plan, and then, as his mentor would say, a plan A and plan B!

The plan was that once they were in Earth's orbit, Jayne would pilot the shuttle ship to Bubba's home, and Bubba would go inside to retrieve the prize while Jayne guarded the front door in case of any surprises. They would then get aboard the shuttle and head back to the starship.

The time between the jumps went fast as they were now approaching the second space fold event.

With about fifteen minutes before the last jump began, Utago motioned Bubba to come to him. He was located in a spot that made it impossible for Jayne to hear what was said besides having very little view of them both.

What Jayne could see was Utago giving Bubba something that he then put into his pocket. She assumed it was some type of weapon but really could not be certain what it was.

The shuttle was tiny compared to the other crafts Bubba had ridden in. Jayne could see the apprehension on his face, which made her smile and speak.

"Now, Captain Jones, are you worried about my driving? She asked with a giggle.

"Not at all, just…" and then it looked like he was struggling for the right words, "…wondering if I will fit." He finished that with a big smile, which made Jayne smile back.

One of the things that amazed Bubba was how they all seemed to know how to drive each other's vessels. He compared it to computer operating systems that can be different and yet have many similarities. Most of the people he met had been trained in multiple systems and operated them with ease.

Once they were inside the craft, they sat in elbow-to-elbow conditions. Jayne explained that this was like a sports car, being very small and fast but really useless on long journeys.

After she hit a few buttons and worked the monitor, holographic controls emerged, which she then used. It had maps stored within its systems of Earth but also could tap into Earth's map systems.

Bubba's house became a 3D model, and Jayne picked an area within his backyard to land in. After that, the ship handled the entire trip and landing. Bubba thought that, with a little training, he could fly her.

It was around 7:30 pm. Twilight was the light at hand, yet quickly fading to black. Maybe it was the lighting conditions or just the last weeks of Bubba's life, but it all seemed foreign, like he was just a visitor, and all of this was not really his home. Even though they were in the back of his property and heading to the front door, Bubba decided he wanted to get the mail.

His mailbox was overflowing, and he knew he should not be getting his mail when he saw an envelope from Brand Wright. Then he remembered how Brand always told him to write a goodbye letter to the people he cared about in case you don't make it back from a mission.

Their last mission to Mars must have been when Brand sent it, just before they left. Bubba then felt bad that he had not reciprocated the act. He put it in his jacket pocket and then quickly moved to the front door. Jayne had already pulled her gun out, which Bubba tried to get her to put away.

She argued, "You need to move, Captain Jones. I feel trouble is coming." To Bubba, she now looked like a cat. Her natural slim figure stretched out and moved around nimbly, yet ready to pounce when needed.

As he approached the door, his biggest fears were confirmed. His front door was open. The frame was in tack, so either someone used a key or picked it. Now Bubba was moving like time was the last thing he had.

His next huge disappointment was when his secret library room was found. He felt it was more than one person who had invaded and desecrated his most special place. And just for spite, had left the bookshelf that operated by rotating from its center open by 5 inches.

Now his heart became heavy, his movements slowed down, scared to find out the last ultimate defeat. Did they find his secret room behind the back of the closet within his secret library room?

3

THE CONFRONTATION

Pierce contacted Sam Smith regarding the actions happening at Bubba Jones' home. Pierce, who had traveled to Florida, was informed by NASA that a ship had landed at the target's location, plus other details. He was well aware of Sam's personal interest in this case and was calling to confirm what actions should take place.

"Sir, Bubba Jones has returned to his home with an unknown woman. They arrived in his backyard using a space shuttle. What actions do you want taken?"

Sam had been more distracted in thought than usual, which is saying a lot since he would spend hours in deep contemplation.

"Contact Colonel Bolt to oversee the operation. I want them detained for an interview. Make sure to bring all their possessions with them. Contact me immediately once this is done." With that, Sam disconnected from the call. It was not said, but if Pierce had messed this up, he would have been replaced.

Sam started to doubt Pierce's loyalty. The thing that bothered him was he really could not put his finger on why. That troubled him the most, as he was not able to understand the logic behind his thoughts. Sam also developed a high regard for Bolt's opinions, which influenced him.

Hunches or gut feelings are not the same as a Reality Benders' abilities, but they are real, and so many things are not truly understood as to why they work.

Pierce contacted a team for the project. It consisted of eight people trained as a unit that could quickly reorganize themselves as needed for a positive completion of the mission. They were men and women with the highest training who had proven themselves and were in their prime.

Pierce then contacted Colonel Bolt. It was arranged that they would meet in a war room to oversee the operations. The basic elements of a war room consisted of many monitors numbering from 12 to 24. Also, there would be at least three to five large monitors. The room is soundproof and deploys high technologies between all resources involved.

That type of room was available within the building that Bolt worked in. Its location was in the second basement. Bolt arrived first and had already connected with the team deployed for the mission.

Pierce who, like Sam Smith, was usually short with words, gave a nod of acknowledgment that Bolt was there. His full attention was on the monitors. One of the large monitors was a fixed camera on the front door. Another large screen had a view of the back door. In most homes, that would suffice, yet Bubba's home had so many angles that actually finding the back door was a judgment call.

Eight of the little cameras had feeds showing each of the soldiers, with below the cameras displaying their vital signs. The team had set up a perimeter mostly around the front door with two soldiers at the back.

It was a moonless night that quickly turned black. The blackness draped everything in an invisible magic cloth. Even with that and the distance they were from the home, which was still far away, Jayne was becoming agitated. This was observed with the night vision binoculars they were using.

It seemed to Jayne that Captain Jones had been gone for quite some time. She was annoyed at herself for not marking the start of his entering the home. By the time she had looked at her watch, it was now stretching into ten minutes plus, but it really was longer than that.

While she was waiting outside, her senses detected a change in the environment. Being trained as a soldier and having combat experience prior to this, all that can be said is you get a feeling that things are not right. It may be the air or sounds, maybe a smell or a shadow that seems to move, just little things that by themselves mean nothing, but at this moment, they are all shouting red flags.

Jayne's weapon, which was already out, was based on energy projection, electricity controlled by a laser light. It was standard in the galaxy as weapons go. She set the device to have a wide focus with less destruction force, which would disable an enemy without killing them. Also, her aim would not be as critical, being it had a wide spread of discharge.

It was the type of night that no matter how long you were out there, your eyes never adjusted to the blackness.

As more time marched on in a very slow fashion, Jayne's instincts were that trouble was minutes away. She wanted to yell for her Captain to get moving, yet her training told her to keep silent in the dark night. Not to give her position away, but in that regard, she moved behind some large bushes that were near the door.

There was only one microphone connected directly to the leader of the squad preparing to apprehend Bubba and Jayne. That microphone was between Pierce and Bolt, Bolt being in command of the operation.

The team communicated directly with each other per their personal communicators, having their own jargon that few understood.

Pierce leaned forward towards the mic and said, "Let there be light."

With that, three bright field lights were cranked on, bringing the night to day. It was way too bright to be of any comfort on who it showed on. Jayne instinctively crouched lower and, with her eyes closed, heightened her hearing senses. She knew the light would blind her if they were open, also knowing that she would fire her weapon as the sounds around her became louder in the direction away from the front door.

Then, the commands came from the other side of the light to, "Drop your weapons," and, "Come out with your hands up!"

Just after that, the front door burst open. It was kicked open from inside the home so forcefully that the sound and violence of its opening commanded everyone's attention.

"Turn that light down now!" This was said with a deep voice, tone, and an anger that would not be denied some type of action. Jayne and few others had ever heard Bubba angry. It had taken about five seconds before it was obeyed.

Colonel Bolt gave the order, and they were lowered to levels that were useful without bringing pain to any who were there. Partly because of his friendship with Bubba, they had spent time together during the Antarctica incident. The other part was his disdain for Pierce. It was then that Bubba made his appearance from the empty open-door space through the doorframe and into the light. The action gave him an even bigger appearance than he already had.

Now, the remaining two soldiers from the back door were with the six in front of Bubba and Jayne.

Bubba was a big man and always knew how to use it to his advantage. He was not a fighter by nature. All big men can be intimidating if they want to be. Bubba's next words were also commanding in how he said them. There is a way of asking a question that demands to be answered.

"Who is in charge?" This question was more a demand to be answered and nothing less than that person will do. That was the feeling Jayne had when she heard it. She admired his courage but questioned his tactics as he was fully exposed with no weapon or protection. Bubba had one hand in his pocket and seemed to be trying to get something. In his other hand was an aluminum briefcase about 6 inches wide handcuffed to his wrist.

Colonel Bolt snapped at the microphone, his personal phone number, "Tell Mr. Jones to call me." The leader followed orders while Jayne and Bubba were surrounded by his team in a half circle with their weapons aimed at them.

Bubba used a video connection and was surprised at who appeared there.

He started with, "Now, is this any way to say hello? Mighty un-friendly, sir. I will just be on my way, and all is forgiven."

Colonel Bolt had a serious face and attitude as he replied.

"Mr. Jones, Bubba, this is not a game. We need to talk, and you need to surrender now."

Bubba responded with the following statement.

"Sir, we are at a stalemate. You, Sam Smith, heck the whole country owes him. If anyone should understand, it is you! I need to leave right now."

Bolt knew in his heart he was right. Being a soldier all his life, orders will always override feelings, and he responded.

"Bubba, you are right, but this is bigger than Brand. The truth is that this is not a stalemate, and you are not Brand Wright. Even he would not be able to talk or shoot his way out of this."

Jayne was studying Bubba. He showed no fear nor anger at what was just said. It seemed he was always weak in command, but now, when it really mattered, his strength matched the task.

"Colonel Bolt, this does not have to end badly." As he said that, he was looking more towards the sky than the threat in front of him. Time had seemed to stop. Each second felt like a minute. Jayne was seconds away from pulling the trigger on her weapon and, for the first time, wishing Utago was with them.

Then, the dark night sky changed. Something was there that could not be seen but could be observed because of the lack of stars. What was seen brought everyone's attention to themselves, but not in a good way. Red laser lights were pointed at each person from different areas of the night sky. If that was not amazing enough, the light that shined down from the dark night curved at the bottom to meet the victim's chest.

No matter where or how they moved, the lights stayed on them. It was controlled by computers and could reconfigure the light faster than human action could move.

There were only two people to whom the light was not attached: Jayne and Bubba.

Bubba, now looking into his phone, said, "I am leaving." With that, he looked at Jayne and nodded his head so she could come with him. They would be exposing their backs to the enemy, and Jayne was reluctant in her facial expression to go.

Bubba then said to her, "It will be fine." With his look, she experienced a new feeling, the feeling of trust in his words. Like all her fears could be disregarded. That she would abandon her knowledge and go with him in faith.

Jayne walked over to him and turned her back as they started to retrace their steps to the shuttle.

Pierce grabbed the microphone and said in an excited voice, "Take the shot."

Bolt responded quickly and forcefully, taking the microphone back to shout his orders.

"Counter that order!" Yet before his first word came out, all the soldiers' screens went blank. Their life signs below the screens all went to flat lines. At that moment, he wanted to kill Pierce, and he thought about how to do it. Then sanity returned, and Bolt just stared at him.

For Pierce's part, he was not fazed at all. He just stared back like what are you going to do, old man.

Utago knew that the transmitter he gave Bubba might come in handy. Also, being able to monitor the conversation between Pierce and Bolt, he was ready if needed, which was the case. Utago was the smartest of his current companions, and his reflexes were quicker than those of humans. He also was impressed with Bubba and his coolness under pressure. It reminded him of Brand and why they were risking their lives for him. It was a worthy cause.

A flash happened behind Jayne and Bubba. It was brief, only lasting two seconds. The aftermath will live lifetimes. Bubba was not emotionally prepared for what he saw when turning around. There were the eight soldiers, all dead with holes in their chests. There was a bit of smoke and smell.

Bubba was frozen in shock. Just a moment ago, they were all alive, worrying about the things we all worry about. Now gone, gone forever, and for the first time, he appreciated Brand's pain. He remembered how Brand lamented about people being around him and dying, how he felt guilty. Bubba remembered telling him that it was not his fault. Things happen, and he just happened to be there at the time.

Bubba's thoughts went to what had just happened. If he had surrendered, none of this would have occurred. He had caused it, and now, like Brand, people were dying just being around him. That was why Brand wanted to be alone, to stop the cycle.

Jayne, for her size was very strong among her other features. She was pulling Bubba along to the shuttle, which was not easy considering Bubba's size. She had looked at the same scene Bubba had viewed with no reactions at all.

Being a soldier and seeing many others die before this event, that is what happens. If you are alive, be happy for that fact and move on, were her thoughts at that moment.

Finally, a few yards before the shuttle, Bubba returned to his old self. He had a sad look that also showed determination to see this venture out. No words were spoken until he was back on their starship.

The starship was now more home to Bubba than the house he just left. Upon arrival, it became the safe haven that his old home used to be. His mind flooded with what just happened and also how he was processing it all.

The first thing he noted was the change in the relationship between Jayne and Utago. As soon as Jayne saw Utago she rushed up to him, jumping towards his chest as one of his large, strong arms gently scooped her up.

She hugged him and, looking into his eyes, said, "Thank you!"

Bubba was feeling quite differently than that, starting with, "Why did you do that?" It was not said in anger being a true question. Yet there was a vibration that Bubba was angry. Maybe it was sadness. It was not gratitude.

Utago clearly knew where Bubba was coming from. What was becoming clear to everyone was how smart and important he was to their survival and the success of the mission. If he had not given the emergency transmitter to Bubba and told him to use it if trouble arrived, they would have been captured at his home's front door.

He also had the starship close, so it would only take minutes to get there. His expert knowledge of the ship's weaponry systems, plus all the other systems, saved the day. For most, that would have been enough that he had saved their lives.

Right now, that was not enough, and Utago understood why. So, without saying anything, he flicked a few controls, and on the sound system, the conversation between Pierce and Bolt played.

All that Utago said was, "I waited."

Then, as a follow-up, he said, "I am faster." Which was completed with a smile.

It was then that Bubba thanked him, excusing himself that he needed time to process all that had happened. Jayne would work on finding out the Nevermore location, and Utago, well, he was the hero of the day.

Both Jayne and Utago wanted to see what was in the briefcase still handcuffed to Bubba's arm, but neither said anything.

4

—

LETTER FROM THE PAST

Sam Smith had just finished his call from Colonel Bolt, who was quite upset with Pierce and almost demanded something be done. Sam was not an impulsive person. Quite the opposite. He could think out a problem from many different perspectives just to make sure he analyzed it correctly before he applied his solution.

He contacted Pierce to review what happened. Sam did not reveal that Colonel Bolt had called.

Sam began by saying, "I am disappointed in the outcome at Mr. Jones' home, explain why it happened?"

Pierce was always in control of his emotions and did not show any signs of fear or worry with Sam's statement, almost to the point that it felt not normal. Sam was a very powerful man and disappointing him was not a good move for anyone.

Pierce replied, "I am sure you are aware of the facts. The prize was walking away. It was worth taking the shot."

Sam was a practical man. What Pierce said was true, and his actions were correct, even if the outcome was disastrous.

Sam continued, "The search of the home was your responsibility."

After what was a very long minute in silence, Sam said, "Dismissed."

————

The captain's room on the starship was extraordinary, unlike most other areas of the ship, and it was decorated with many different high-end types of woods featuring walnut, cherry, and mahogany. The style was based on the staterooms of the late 1800s. Once in there, you would be hard-pressed to know you were on a starship or any type of ship.

Then Bubba thought about it. Of course, once you get used to being on a starship, it is even better to be able to forget you are on one. That is exactly what the room did for him.

Now that the excitement was over, he pulled out the letter Brand had sent him just before they left for Mars. He called them "Goodbye letters," making it easier for those left after if you don't return.

Bubba opened the letter and studied each word it contained.

"Dear Bubba, the fact that you're reading this letter and I have not pulled it out of your mailbox means at least I am no longer on Earth. Probably, it means I am dead or close to death or worse. So, before I go into all I want to say, let's go over the possibilities above. If I am off Earth, that is fine, and death is just that. The last two predicaments are the hard ones. If I am close to death or worse, please don't risk yourself or others in rescuing me. I have spoken many times about how many I carry, and the worst would be for you or others to add to that pile.

Now, to the good stuff, your friendship meant so much to me. My words are weak, and your actions were always strong. You're a great man, which is pretty extraordinary given what goes on in these times. You never let your wealth affect you, and you are kind. Please don't lose those qualities.

Thank you for all the great times, for saving my life more times than I can count."

The next section brought tears running down Bubba's cheeks.

"Please take care of Sweetbull. She can be a thing, but her heart is so wonderful. I promise she will love you like you have never experienced love before.

Now, my friend, I am on the next stage of my journey. Please take good care of yourself and Sweetbull.

Your friend, Brand."

When Bubba read Sweetbull's name, thoughts of Brand and her playing, eating and napping together flooded his mind. The love they had for each other shown in so many ways.

Then, there is this mission he was commanding. It was exactly the opposite of what Brand wanted. A dying man's wishes have a long tradition that commands them to be honored. Now, he had to make so many choices that affected so many others. Should he honor his best friend's last wishes and let him die? Already trying to save him had cost eight people their lives, and he knew there would be more if he continued.

Bubba thought to himself, should he tell his companions about Brand's last wishes?

There were just too many choices, which made his head feel hot like it was on fire. He recalled how stressful his first day on Mars was and how Brand always said that after a good night's sleep, things become clearer, easier, and better.

Bubba had not removed the briefcase that was attached to his wrist via the handcuff. That was a decision he had already made. It would not be removed until they were back on the Nevermore. Even then, it was not until Brand was in sight.

Bubba had already made a plan and a backup plan. Yet the doubt about the righteousness of the venture now became a new burden he would have to carry. As he tried to get comfortable in what was a marvelous bed, it was hard getting used to the big briefcase that was in the way.

Sleep always has a way of winning the battle, and he fell into a deep sleep. Sadly, it was not peaceful.

When Bubba awoke, he found Utago in the command center, and Jayne was sleeping. This was a bit disappointing as he wanted to give each of their gifts together.

Bubba, looking directly at Utago, said, "Utago, this is a book that Brand wrote and published. It is his author's copy, with his personalized blue stamp, and it is signed and dated. I know he would want you to have it." With that, he handed him the book titled "SUBJECT 9," which Utago received as if it were a sacred object.

Utago's voice seemed to break up, for it sounded different than it usually did.

"Thank you," was all he could manage to say. It was his eyes and how he handled the book that made a statement. Just as Bubba was going to say, always keep it close as it is a unique possession, Utago forcefully said.

"I keep on me, always!" It was not said but shouted, and with that, he put it inside his shirt pocket. Bubba did not even know there was a pocket there.

Now, Jayne had entered the room to find out what was happening.

"Perfect, now I can give you your gift from Brand," Bubba said with a big smile.

Jayne, for the first time, seemed taken aback by that statement. Maybe it was because she expected a gift from Brand given to her by Brand himself. She was not moving, appearing frozen in thought, which quickly became an awkward moment.

Bubba reacted to it with, "Promise you're going to like it." Then, he motioned her to sit down as he sat on a chair across from her.

"This gift from Brand has been in his family for over 100 years. It was his great-grandfather's watch. Brand had a special love for his grandmother, who had been gifted the watch by her father. Then, she directly gave it to Brand when he was a young man. He had kept it secure for many decades, and I know he would want you to have it."

After Bubba had said all that, Jayne's response was typical of Jayne.

"So why do you have it? Did he give it to you, and now you are giving it to me?"

Bubba was hurt inside yet did not show it. As he was sitting directly across from her and looking straight into her eyes, he responded.

"Brand is my best friend, and I am his. In Florida, when you are gone, your home has a way of losing many of its possessions. Brand like many others, have family that live far away. Before any family makes it down, the homes end up empty of almost everything of value, like vultures in the desert, stripped and cleaned.

Brand gave me this, one of his most valuable possessions for safeguarding. He lived each day like it could be his last and wanted this, his treasured watch protected." Bubba was not done. He just paused to finish what he wanted done.

"Brand told me to give it to someone who would value it the way he does. Knowing how much he wants to thank both of you for what you are doing for him, I picked two gifts, one for each of you. I only ask that you carry them with you and value them the way Brand did."

Jayne now looked like someone who was ashamed of her words.

Bubba picked up on it and said quickly, "It was a good question, and I am glad you asked it." With that, he handed her a very old pocket watch. It was created in 1834 by the Elgin company, and a testimony to them was that it still worked. It had a front that opened to show the watch face, which was finely decorated with small pearls around the numbers. They were connected with little gold dots on a white background, making the face extremely ornate. The back also opened, and the top had an oval-shaped circle for attaching a chain.

Jayne who usually wore sweaters that rose to her neck, also had a tube-like chain around her neck. It was made of some type of metal material that had a clasp that seemed to appear and disappear. She attached the watch to it and then put both items back into her sweater.

Jayne said, "Captain Jones, I will wear this at all times. This necklace is very strong, and I will never give it away."

Bubba now seemed very pleased with himself. He started to look like his old self before the visit to Earth. Without saying anything, he opened his arms with Jayne, giving him a big hug.

It appeared that the Nevermore was somewhere near the edge of the galaxy as if it was trying to hide. Their location was far from that area, and it would take many jumps to get there. Until they were relatively close, the exact math needed for the jumps was not critical.

Jayne informed both Bubba and Utago that it would take at least a week to just get there. Then, more time until they locate the ship. This news obviously brought down the feeling of happiness regarding the presents, but the team was still in good spirits.

During the first few days, Bubba was doing boot camp on how to run the ship, from flying to communications. Weapon systems and life support were also included.

Jayne was actively checking where she believed the Nevermore should be and working on the next space fold needed. Utago was reading his book, SUBJECT 9. He was wearing what looked like white cloth gloves. Utago was always surprising Bubba. He was so big yet also smart and fast in reflexes. Yet there was the sensitive side, the way he dreamed of doing big things and now wearing gloves so as not to damage a single page from his treasured book.

During this entire time, Bubba refused to take off the handcuff attached to the briefcase attached to his wrist. This caused a bit of awkwardness, which Bubba addressed with the following statement:

"I know that you both want to see the contents within this briefcase. Also, you feel hurt that I constantly keep it attached to my wrist. I trust you both with my life and ask that you both trust me regarding this."

This statement took both Jayne and Utago by surprise as it addressed the elephant in the room. Both stated it was fine, yet that awkwardness remained.

In Bubba's mind, it was amazing how fast one can get used to a disability. Lugging the briefcase around as he ate, slept, and did all his other tasks, it started to become his natural state.

On the fifth day of their journey to find the Nevermore, the distress call arrived. It amazed Bubba how many things were similar on Earth as they were to the galaxy. In this case, when in close contact with a ship in distress and if they have activated their emergency distress call, then it announces itself to all ships in the vicinity.

There was no denying that type of call. The special warning sound, which was very similar to the air raid sounds used in World War II, went screaming off. Followed by a voice announcing the ship's name and location, ending with a plea for help.

They were located in a very empty area of space, considering that most of the space was empty to begin with.

Bubba was in the command center, he loved sitting on the captain's chair and immersing himself in that role. Jayne was also there working on the next-to-last jump as the alarm went off. By the time she looked at Bubba, he was already staring at her.

Bubba began, "We must try to help."

Just then, Utago walked in, moving close to Jayne. They were both in agreement that the mission must come first as if they had the same mindset without speaking, and they grouped together to bolster their position.

Jayne began, "Captain Jones, I understand your good nature wants to help, but the mission to save CW comes first."

Then, correcting herself, she continued, "Brand, he is so close to death. Every second we delay may spell his doom."

Utago started after she ended, "Brand first!"

Bubba just then was having a flashback to when Brand and himself were going to get his DeLorean car. Right before they would have arrived, there was a girl missing, and Brand was determined to save her. Bubba felt it was hopeless. He only wanted to get his car.

Then his mind went to the saying that to truly understand someone, you have to walk in their shoes. This trip was providing revelations about his friend and himself that could only be obtained by this journey he was on. The similarities between what happened to Brand and what he is now going through are uncanny. He was still feeling very guilty about the eight soldiers who died trying to stop them on Earth. If he could help these people in distress, maybe it would balance things a bit.

Also, the fact that Brand had special abilities that Bubba and most others didn't had made things easier for him, yet Bubba's mind was made.

Bubba looked at his fellow companions and said, "We are not just going to save Brand, but to honor him. When we are successful, he will want to know our complete adventures in getting it done. I know he would want their rescue to come first and that he would never…" Then, with a long pause, "…look at us the same way if we do nothing."

That speech touched both Jayne and Utago to their hearts. Bubba always seems smarter than he appeared, were their thoughts. Neither had further arguments to make, so it was decided that Utago and Bubba would check out the distressed ship.

Jayne, looked at Bubba and stated, "You know you are going to have to take off the briefcase to use the suit."

Bubba, without a thought, replied, "No problem." And with that, he used the key and unlocked the handcuff attached to his wrist.

This was strange in that he had resisted removing it no matter what the circumstances before and now completed the act without hesitation.

Jayne said, "Well, I will keep it safe." Bubba just shook his head up and down with an affirmative grin.

5

THE RESCUE

The ship was not far from their location and was quite large. These things can be hard to judge, but to Bubba, it was much smaller than the Nevermore yet bigger than Dragonfly's starship. Compared to their starship, it was much bigger.

Their suits allowed them to move through space and they went to the doors that were blinking from the ship ahead of them. They must have activated those doors after the distress call to make it easier for someone to help.

After touching a large green button, which made Bubba grin at how universal some things are, the door opened, and they were in a chamber that was separated from the ship. Once the outer door was sealed shut, the front door opened.

They communicated with each other and Jayne. All were quiet, showing good training and restraint.

Bubba was getting used to the look of starships, and this one was quite similar. It almost did not seem to matter who made them, as they were quite similar in the end. There were always differences, but there was nothing that could not be overcome.

There was no gravity, so they were doing a swimming motion while using their jet packs that were attached to their suits. They did arm movements mostly, so they did not hit any walls. All electronics were non-operational, with only the distress call and doors working.

Less than ten minutes on the ship, the dead bodies started to show up. Scattered in different areas like autumn leaves. Once alive and doing life things, now just lying crumpled up and floating in place.

There was no one left alive. They died as their life support systems stopped. The ship itself had shut down those programs. Then there were people in space suits trying to outlast whatever problem that had befallen them. After a time, those systems became depleted, finishing what the ship had started.

Making matters worse was a total system failure in all the systems aboard. This also included the emergency escape ships. A total technology failure pointing to only one thing.

Space is like the great oceans of Earth, unforgiving in its punishment while being so beautiful. These were the thoughts of Bubba as he saw so much death.

Utago, who had been leading the way, as they were keeping an eye on each other, turned and motioned that they should go.

"We go."

Bubba felt a sense of urgency in Utago's voice. Maybe it was the communication device, yet it felt like it was there.

When Bubba tried to contact Jayne to let her know they were returning, the communications failed. It was then that he knew they were in trouble. At least the airlock was right ahead. This time, no lights were on, and it did not open, making them stuck inside the death ship.

Utago, with excitement in his voice, said, "Follow…" His voice ended as it broke off from Bubba's speaker in his suit. Now, their communications had broken down. This was much more than just a coincidence. They were under attack.

Bubba followed Utago, who was looking for something he had finally found. It was a large observation window. He pulled out of one of his big pockets what looked like grey mud. For a moment, it looked like he was judging how much to use as he pulled a piece of it off and put it back into his pocket. He attached the rest to the window. It was easily attached, like it was very sticky.

Utago turned, looking at Bubba, and with his hand, motioned him to come towards him. Then, what looked like a smartwatch, which Bubba never realized he had, Utago pushed some buttons, and the glass started to change.

It appeared to have lines that turned into patterns, making it harder to see through. It was fracturing at a molecular level. When the process was over, it turned into millions of little pieces that were slowly moving apart.

Utago grabbed Bubba's arm and slowly moved from the death ship through the now-defunct observation window into space. They were safe from the ship, but now their suits' life support systems were failing. They had minutes to get back into their starship, but unfortunately, it was not in sight.

During their escape, they had exited to the left of the ship while Jayne and their ship were under and to the right of them.

In normal circumstances, this would not be a major problem. They would just coordinate between parties until they met. This was not a normal circumstance. Communications were down, and they had less than 3 minutes to find their ship.

In Bubba's mind, they were doomed. Three minutes goes by very quick when your life depends on it. He was proud that he was taking it for what it was. Knowing your end is coming and not crying or pleading to someone, anyone, for help. To man up and meet your end with dignity and courage.

Then his thoughts went to Utago, who was still holding his right arm. He could see his face as they were moving to where he thought the ship would be. It occurred to him that maybe Utago could hold his breath much longer than a human. He looked focused but not scared.

His thoughts of Jayne made Bubba smile. She was safe as long as she stayed away from the death ship. One thought lead to another, which eventually lead to Brand. He wondered what Brand would do in this situation.

There was less than a minute left of oxygen within the suit. Utago still looked like they were going to make it. Bubba was now thinking about his life and how, after meeting Brand, it had become a new life. He was happy that he had experienced Mars, Antarctica, and so many other places and things.

With less than 30 seconds of oxygen, the unbelievable happened. Jayne was coming right at them so fast that Bubba thought now they would die by being run over.

The loading deck door opened while she spun the ship around, literally scoping them in. Then, the loading deck door closed while she stopped the starship to check on her companions.

Utago was still pulling Bubba along. They immediately left the loading dock, and once the doors were closed, they ripped off the suits they were wearing.

Utago was still moving like time was of the essence, but Bubba thought the emergency was over. Jayne was confused but had a soldier's instinct that trouble was present.

Jayne asked, "What is the problem? What did you find?"

Before Bubba could speak, as he had a suspicion of what was going on, Utago responded.

"No time! Follow me." He led them to the emergency evacuation room. There were the pods providing an escape from their ship.

"Get in."

Bubba now was just following orders, whether it was Jayne or Utago giving them. He lay down in the pod, which was about 4 feet wide and 12 feet long.

The builders of starships, or other ships for that matter, knew there were many unknown hazards in space. Many precautions are built into ships to combat possible termination scenarios.

One problem is a complete system failure, where no electronics are working. Escape pods have a manual deployment as long as there is one person left on board to operate it. This setup provided an escape from the ship, but no one person could utilize it. Another safety precaution is to try and predict any and all issues that may arise.

Utago was now looking at Jayne and barked, "You, get in!"

Jayne looked at Utago, saying, "Hold on one minute." With that, she went running out of the room.

When time is the most important factor, waiting can be an eternity. Within 10 seconds of Jayne leaving the room, all the power within the ship went off. Now, time seemed to go on forever as they waited for Jayne's return.

Bubba had many questions, yet now did not seem to be the right time. Utago, being annoyed at how long Jayne was taking, canceled those thoughts.

Finally, she returned with Bubba's briefcase. She laid it on his chest, saying, "Save CW!"

With that, she jumped into the last escape pod and then, looking at Utago, said, "Thank you." After a momentary pause, she added in another language, something else, with Utago shaking his head up and down.

There was a big switch that looked like the switches on a big fuse box. The two switches were next to each other, with the pods on the left and right, respectively. Utago, with one switch in each hand, pulled both at the same time.

There was a roar and an air rush as the two pods escaped the starship and headed into the black night.

———

Utago was pleased, and he allowed himself to enjoy it for a few seconds. Then, his attention went to his own survival. He ran around the ship grabbing all sorts of different items. Many electronic devices plus also as much food packets as would fit in the escape tube. Making it looked like Utago was on a scavenger hunt.

There was one last option to get off the ship. It would only be prolonging the inevitable end.

Utago thoughts were, *the final end will come to us all, and each day, we do what we can to prolong it.*

There was an escape tube that had a circumference of 5 feet, and its length was 12 feet. It was the last chance of survival and was used if the ship is over a planet when the escape pods were inoperable or being used. With straps inside to hold people or things, it had a maximum air supply of 12 hours. There was not much on life support or communications, but it did have some mechanism to slow down once it encountered the planet's gravity.

Utago was throwing many things into it to the point it was a tight fit when he finally settled in. He wanted to deploy a stay-away beacon and set the starship to self-destruction, yet everything within the ship was not working.

The escape tube did have a manual start option within the tube. It was a last-chance option, and few security protocols were attached to its deployment. The problem was he would have little time to be found. Really, he was just prolonging the end.

Bubba felt like he was lying in a contoured bed. There was a video screen above him with some buttons below the screen. Then, the feeling of being totally alone in space enveloped his being. It felt like he was an ant in the desert, with no friends and no chance of survival. A crushing force upon his spirit, which, now that the prior actions were finished, started its campaign. For a moment, the hopelessness overwhelmed him.

The video screen coming to life brought Bubba back to better thoughts. It was Jayne on the screen.

"Captain Jones, I am going to help you set up your rescue beacon and hibernation program. Are you ready to begin?"

"No, no, I am not. I am not a captain, and I have ruined everything."

"Captain Bubba Jones, did you think all your decisions would be right, that everything would go as planned? You are the captain. You made good choices. You were right that CW would have stopped to help. He is in a time capsule, and the Nevermore has been around for decades. Once we get rescued, the mission will resume, and you will still be Captain."

Bubba was surprised at how well Jayne had taken all that had just transpired. She was so upset about how many jumps to get to Earth, now so accepting of all his failures.

Bubba then asked, "What about Utago? Will he make it?"

Jayne responded as a seasoned soldier who had lost many in her young life, "No, he will die. He gave his life for us to complete this mission."

Bubba was now very somber. "How did you find us so fast when we were stuck in space outside the death ship?"

Jayne, feeling a bit bad, replied, "I never really trusted Utago, so I placed a hidden tracker on him. I activated it when I lost contact with you. It died about 10 seconds after you exited the craft. I followed the last reading at full speed, and you know the rest."

Jayne was now re-focused on getting Bubba ready for hopefully their short hibernation in the huge emptiness of black space.

"Captain Jones, it is very easy to activate the hibernation controls. The rescue beacon will automatically activate unless it is disabled. I need you to follow my directions, and after you are set, I will activate mine. Don't be alarmed when the mist fills your pod. It's just the hibernation gas. The reason Utago sent us out together at the same time is so when one is found, the other will be too."

Then she went through the steps needed, which was just hitting one button and one more button to confirm. It really was very easy, and Bubba was glad she warned him about the mist.

With one arm wrapped around the briefcase, he went into hibernation mode.

6

DRAGONFLY AND UTAGO

One may ask, what is in a name? It is not the word but what you make of that word that counts. Some names are so filled with things, great and bad. And who is to judge, for so many times the story is skewed. Leaning to glorify and demonize the parties involved, depending on the writer.

Dragonfly was the name they gave her; love and caring were not provided. She was created and treated as property. Genetically blended from human and octopus plus other life forms to be the best of all possible combinations.

Yet, like each of us, she was so much more than what could be observed or known. Yes, she was a genius at levels that are hard to imagine. How can the average truly understand that type of greatness?

And yes, she had deep emotions that no one cared to ask her about. It was always about solving puzzles, fixing problems, and trying to get new things out of her. Did they really believe she would give them answers to help them control things even more than they already do?

In her mind, it was crazy that the masses did not see the obvious. That they were being used as slave labor compared to what they produced.

She escaped from their prison, which they called an HLC, a high-level containment facility. Then, through different means that were not directly connected to her, she tried to convey information that she thought would enlighten people.

Sadly, Dragonfly failed, or you might say the people failed to appreciate or understand her warnings. Either way, nothing much changed. Yet smart people always learn from their mistakes.

She has a photographic memory with thousands of books memorized. Her abilities in languages have no comparison.

Geniuses at her level are always alone. There lies the problem, her great intelligence did not remove that curse from her life. It only accentuated that condition. Where others would believe that maybe in the future they would meet their other half, in her case, there was no other half by design. Her creation was great science and pure accident combined, that could never be replicated.

Then, her thoughts went to the people who made a difference in her life. First on that list was Sam Smith. He was her father and mother, the man who was behind her great abilities and her terrible conditions of life on Earth.

Right next to him was Brand Wright. A man with many names, aka Plutoneus, Subject 9, CW, and Mr. X. For some people, one name is not enough. She thought there was something special about him. He really had no power, yet his presence commanded attention. Brand had saved her life once but had also hurt her many times.

There was when he convinced her to go for help when it was just leading her into a private prison. Then, he appeared again to ruin her revenge against Sam Smith. If that were not enough, he showed up on Mars just when she was ready to consume a potion of extended life via the Philosopher's Stone. His presence on Mars started an attack that ruined that, plus major portions of the planet's buildings.

If that was not enough, Brand affected her more. Utago adored Dragonfly and called her his Queen. Once he met Brand, he was so impressed with his bravery that Dragonfly had lost her biggest fan and only real friend.

No matter how much money or wisdom you may have, it does not stop loneliness. Dragonfly really didn't care about the starship she had lent Bubba and Utago. They were supposed to return it after the fight between Brand and General Max. That fight had come and ended with no ship returning.

Now, she would find her lost starship. That is what she was telling herself. The truth was she was looking for her old friends.

And then there was Bubba, the nicest man she had ever been acquainted with. Even Bubba was changing being around Brand so much. She felt a special type of love for Bubba. The type that a mother has for her children. His innocence regarding so many things.

One aspect of geniuses is they always have more information than the rest of us. This comes about either through their external sources or just the connections their mind reveals that others will not perceive.

The processes Dragonfly used to find her lost starship are beyond trying to explain. It was not easy and had taken much longer than she wanted or expected. On the other hand, it could be compared to finding a drop of water placed in the center of the Pacific Ocean after it had years to travel from that point.

————

Utago was now fighting time, as we all are. It is a fight we will lose, yet some spirits struggle harder against it than others. This applies to all the different forms of life that exist.

Utago's spirit was extremely strong. It was the reason he left his home planet. His species are a strong and smart group. They understand technology and are not gullible. Their inclination was to keep to themselves, and given their size and nature, most others in the galaxy were fine with that.

A few others were adventurers who went with Utago, making him their leader. He was born bigger and smarter than most of his kind. But it was his desire to make a name for himself within the galaxy. Not content to just exist on the planet he was born on, like all explorers, his thoughts were that there was so much more beyond the horizon to see.

With four companions, he started his journey for fame and fortune. It was not long until he met Dragonfly. She was so powerful but not in muscle, in mind. The way she commanded and manipulated all around her to achieve her desires.

Utago decided at that moment that she would be his mentor. His Queen, as he referred to her. He admired knowledge. Being very smart himself, he could tell she was at a totally different level in that area.

Utago thought to himself, that it takes greatness to truly appreciate greatness. The common person can barely recognize it, even if they fell on top of it.

Dragonfly and Utago recognized each other for the special beings they were. His Queen had traveled to Mars to extend her life. That was when he encountered Brand Wright.

To Utago, Brand was fearless, which he praised above intelligence. Utago almost killed Brand when they first met. It was not that Brand was strong or smart. It was his approach and his attitude that made Utago notice him. Then, when Brand went to fight General Max in front of the galaxy, his loyalty to that man was solidified. It was all that Utago dreamed for himself, to fight with glory, regardless of the outcome.

Those thoughts were now going through Utago's mind as the immediate emergency had passed, his escaping the starship. Now, time was the enemy.

He had loaded the escape tube with many different types of supplies. There were the air, heat, and water generators.

He had thrown in as much food as he could find, yet it would never be enough if he was not found quickly.

The most prized machine was a device the galaxy had not seen or even would believe existed. It was called a time crystal, and once known, it would change everything.

The time crystal was created by Dragonfly. It breaks the first two laws of Newton's laws of motion. Utago could see that even Dragonfly was excited by what she had created.

Imagine creating something that has never been seen before, something that would change the universe, and had no one to admire what you had done. Utago, who spent as much time with Dragonfly as she would allow, heard her screaming one day and rushed into her room to render assistance.

Her room at the time was large with a bed and those types of things. Yet, it also had many complicated machines with two big generators that provided exclusive power for her project at hand.

Utago asked, "Queen, you ok?"

Dragonfly looking at him, almost yelling, "I have created the impossible. Something that should not exist yet does because of my brilliance. This, I, am so much better than ok. I call it a time crystal."

She was holding a white crystal that was only an inch long and less than a quarter of an inch wide. It looked very unimpressive, with Utago needing to know more.

Utago asked, "Why name time crystal?"

Dragonfly was in a rare mood, jubilant over her creation, yet she did not have any person in the galaxy to tell. Her mind thinking that Utago is infatuated with me, my one friend in the galaxy. Her general nature was to be secretive, yet this one time, she tried to explain what she had created.

"I started by trying to create a clock with a power source that would not end. All energy dissipates in its transformations. Even the long half-life of radiation is relatively short when thinking in terms of eternity."

Dragonfly could tell by looking at Utago that he was not understanding, so she tried again.

"I have created a perpetual energy machine at the atomic level that defies the physics in which we live. It provides energy without ever needing more to replenish itself while also leaving no after product of the energy it produces."

She then continued, "This is done at the subatomic level and then enlarged while keeping its properties consistent with both levels of reality. It is a new form of matter!"

Utago was still stuck on the name and much of what she told him did not make an impact.

"Should call power crystal," Was all Utago could say.

With that, Dragonfly was already regretting trying to explain something so remarkable to an average mind. To most, just as time and space are connected, so are power and time in Dragonfly's mind. She had created power with unlimited time. It was the next step after Tesla's unlimited power, a battery that will never run out of energy.

Realizing how valuable this was, only two prototype machines were created. One was kept on her main starship, her current vessel. The other was on her much smaller starship she had lent to Utago and Bubba.

The plans for how to create it were strictly in her mind, and nothing was written or recorded about its creation process. This discovery could change everything, everywhere.

Utago, now alone in a tube flying through space, started to realize the impact of Dragonfly's new machine. The likelihood of his survival was extremely small, yet with a time crystal machine, it became much larger.

It did not produce high levels of energy. Dragonfly only used small crystals, and it was created as a proof of concept. Utago had to juggle the use of the air creation with his heater and water machines as the time crystal prototype could only supply each enough energy being used separately. Now, as Utago thought about what Dragonfly had really created, he wondered if the galaxy would ever see it. This is something so new and great that every race and planet would change upon its arrival.

He thought that only two people knew about it, with one of them very close to death. The irony was not lost on him, which just motivated Utago more to somehow survive his current condition.

7

ADAM KNIGHT

Delegati, an Italian word, was the name of their group. In English, it means "Chosen Ones." Sam Smith was their chairman. The group was small, at one time having 11 members, with currently only seven.

Just recently, they wanted to replace Sam. His handling of the Mars incident was considered sloppy and dangerous. After things settled down, it was agreed that he was still the right person to handle whatever may arise.

Now, they were not happy he was leaving Earth, and they demanded that he take a platoon of soldiers just to be on the safe side.

One moment, you're a liability, and the next, a treasured asset.

Before Sam left, there were a few last things he wanted to set in place. When venturing into the galaxy, there can always be unexpected dangers. He called Pierce into his office to set up a meeting with Colonel Bolt.

Sam, looking into Pierce's eyes, asked, "Are you concerned about the fact that I am leaving?"

Without hesitation, Pierce replied, "No." Sam thought he saw a slight grin when Pierce gave his response.

"Set up a meeting with Colonel Bolt in my office for 10 hundred tomorrow. Dismissed."

Then, in an afterthought, he decided to contact Bolt himself with more demands.

Colonel Bolt had picked two candidates to comply with his last conversation with Sam Smith. He tried to explain that people like Sam and Brand Wright can't be replaced, that we all are uniquely special and irreplaceable.

Subject 107, whose birth name was Adam Knight, was thin for 35 years of life. Having a robust beard and long hair, his rebellious spirit was tempered by his self-control and good nature. It appeared that each subject not only had RB abilities but also some special extra gifts.

In Brand Wright's case, he had luck that was more than normal. This had been documented many times within his file throughout the years. The latest example being that General Max did not fully kill him during their battle. The odds were well against that outcome, and most would say he was lucky to survive the encounter.

Adam Knight could see future events, not perfectly, but more than a hunch or logic would predict. His personality was very relaxed, making people comfortable in his presence.

He did not have the training that Brand had, yet once given center stage, some people tended to rise to the occasion. Bolt decided he would start with Subject 107 as his abilities were more suited for the missions Sam Smith would want.

As he was preparing his thoughts, coincidentally, his phone rang with Sam on the other end.

He answered the phone with, "Yes, sir."

"I want to meet Subject 9's replacement. Bring him to the meeting tomorrow."

Bolt was taken by surprise and responded, "Sir, you know, per protocol, it is best if we never meet the subjects directly. When and where is the meeting you are referring to?"

"My office, at 10 hundred tomorrow. Bring- what's his name?"

"Subject 107. Yes, sir," Bolt responded.

Sam disconnected from the conversation first, leaving Bolt shaking his head. He would have to start using Subject 107's real name. The thought just felt abnormal.

That was part of the problem with being around powers greater than your own. Yes, you get to influence them by being the whisper in their ear. On the other hand, being so close makes you an easier pawn in their agendas.

Subject 107 was a manager at a large retail outlet. Bolt would have to pull some strings, meaning contacting someone high up in the chain and having them re-direct Subject 107 to him. The meeting being at 10 in the morning did not leave much time to get everything arranged.

It is a statement of power that comes from the right source or by providing the right motivation, and you can make most people do most things that are desired. Bolt made the call to one very high executive of that company, and after that, he was unaware and really unconcerned with how many other calls past that it had taken to get the required results.

Subject 107, Adam Knight, was waiting at 600 hours in the lobby of the government building from which Colonel Bolt worked. He looked younger than his years and was wearing blue jeans with a pink shirt. His hair was light brown to the point that, in the light, it looked almost red and was long.

It was his striking attitude and friendly approach that instantly put any recipient at ease. In ways, he was the antithesis of Pierce's demeanor.

Bolt introduced himself, "Hello, Adam. I appreciate you taking the time to be here. I want you to meet a friend of mine, and then we will come back here. After that, enjoy the rest of your day. How does that sound?"

Adam, looking at Bolt, extended his right arm with his fist, looking for a fist bump. Then, he smiled and opened his fist for a handshake, saying, "Sounds like fun, especially if he is like you."

Colonel Bolt was caught a bit off guard, then realizing he was just joking and meant no disrespect, answered his handshake with his own and a smile.

"Great. Well, we will be leaving in 10 minutes." With that, he went over to the receptionist, giving her some instructions on something that Adam could not hear.

They proceeded to drive to a small airport where a private jet was waiting for them. Once they boarded the plane, within minutes, they were in the air heading toward Sam Smith.

It was obvious that the plane ride was impressing Adam. Most people will never fly a private jet. There was a feeling of being so special. The built in tables were made with premium woods. The cushions that formed the seats were finely made and contoured for the lucky few who would use them. Yes, there was plenty of legroom.

Adam was looking at Bolt, as the seats were facing each other, when he asked, "Do you mind if I call you by your first name?"

Bolt responded with "Not at all. It is Nicholas, my friends use Nick." As he responded it occurred to him that he really had no friends. His career was everything and had consumed his life.

Then Adam continued the conversation, "I feel this event will change my entire life."

Bolt taking more interest, "How do you feel about that, about your life changing?"

Adam more relaxed said, "I work for a big company. They treat me all right, but I feel I was destined to be more, to do more important things. Riding on this type of plane reinforces those thoughts. You fly a lot on private jets, yes?"

Bolt shook his head positively, almost in a sad way, and answered, "Yes."

Adam looked into Bolt's eyes. "Am I right? This is not ordinary. I am on this type of plane meeting someone extremely important, but for what purpose?"

Now Bolt's answer was the truth and a lie, "You are a very smart, unique person and my friend was just interested in meeting you."

Adam Knight then asked, "Can I talk a selfie with you and me, here in the plane?" Adam had a big smile. Normally Bolt would have declined, yet for whatever reasons, he agreed. Adam had that type of personality, making people feel relaxed and also wanting to comply with his wishes.

They were not in the air for long before they were descending. Traveling at a very high rate of speed, the pilot created a larger arc up and down than standard airplanes would use.

From there, a limousine waited on the tarmac to complete the journey.

It was impressive, regardless of who you were. No tickets, no checkpoints, just speed, luxury, and efficiency.

Once inside Sam's office, everything seemed to slow down. Sam also did not directly introduce himself, though his name was evident in the wood carving sitting on his desk.

"Hello, Mr. Knight. I am sure you are wondering why you are here? Truth is, I have heard such great things about you that I wanted to meet you personally."

Adam, Bolt, and Pierce were silent after that statement was proclaimed.

Then Adam, realizing an awkward moment had arrived, said, "Well, thank you, Mr. Smith. I must say, I don't know what I have done to earn that." Then, out of nowhere, he said, "Would you be interested in picking a Tarot card?" Now, with a big smile, he pulled out a deck that was in his pocket and, after shuffling it three times, handed the deck to Sam.

"Shuffle the deck three times, and then hand the deck back to me."

Sam complied and handed it back to Adam.

Now Adam spread the deck in a straight line with the faces down and told Sam to pick one card. Again, Sam did as directed, pulling a card from the left of the center of the line of cards.

Adam now had everyone's attention as he slowly put his three fingers, excluding his pinky, and rubbed the cards three times in a circular motion.

It was evident from Pierce's eyes that this show was not impressing him. Bolt and Sam's attentions, however, were fixed on the one card that was still face down.

Slowly, Adam turned the card over, revealing The Fool. He could see by the concerned look on Bolt's face that it was a problem. Adam also saw that Pierce had a fast grin, and then his static expression returned. Finally, his attention went to Sam.

Sam did not look upset or happy. Without Sam saying anything, Adam began.

"You are going on a journey, a pilgrimage, following in someone's steps. Leaving your old things and ways behind, traveling light, and finding something great and unexpected. The real problem will be what you have left behind. It is…"

Just at that moment, Pierce's coffee cup hit the floor, and the ceramic container exploded on the hardwood. Everyone's attention was drawn to it and the mess that now lay around and under its aftermath.

Whatever Adam was going to say was lost in that shattered moment. Sam was frozen in thought, and Colonel Bolt gave Pierce a menacing look.

Again, Adam tried to fix the moment by saying, "I hope you have a great trip. Take pictures. I really want to see them."

Sam, now coming back to life, asked, "Would you like to come along?"

8

REUNION

Dragonfly's replacement for Utago had less intelligence than his predecessor and used a standard translator to communicate.

He began with, "Do you want me to board her?"

"No. Follow the emergency signal we picked up earlier." Dragonfly's instincts plus logic dictated her response. Seeing the two ships sitting there, looking perfectly intact, with only one giving off a distressed call, the one she was not looking for.

To her mind, it seemed obvious there was something malignant on one ship, the one sending out the signal that incapacitated the other ship. What that something was right now did not matter. It was something bad, and they were on a rescue mission.

Dragonfly's thoughts were melancholy. Having just found her lost starship dead in space, her only real hope of finding her friends was the escape pods.

When money no longer has any importance, you can buy anything you might desire. Then, no matter who you are, the value of life becomes priceless, especially when your friends or loved ones are involved, she thought.

Dragonfly really missed Utago's adorations and his quizzical mind. She was fond of Bubba's innocence and his good nature regarding life. She wanted them both found.

She would receive half of what she desired.

The escape pod distress signals were not far away and were a much safer bet for finding her friends. Still, they would have to be handled with caution.

Her starship was large by most standards, and it would not be unreasonable to call it huge, considering how many rooms and special functions it possessed. Having the latest in luxury plus security technologies, her ship was well-prepared for most situations.

The ship's safety room consisted of a room with its own air, water, power, and computer systems. Not only that, but besides being a prison, it also was a death area for any who were inside it. If that were not enough, the entire unit could easily be ejected into space if everything went wrong.

Having its own docking bay, the escape pods were directed to its entryway. Once the pods were inside, the room was pressurized. From there, the escape pods' environmental detection system kicked in after registering breathable air and an acceptable temperature.

When Bubba's hatch opened, Jayne was standing above him with care in her eyes. Bubba's first thoughts were how amazing she really was. He had disappointed her every step of their journey together, from how many jumps to get to Earth to trying to help that distressed ship. She never got her way, and yet her devotion to Bubba and the mission never wavered.

"Captain, how are you feeling?" Her voice had true concern in its tone.

The feeling of waking up from an escape pod is similar to recovering from an operation after anesthesia. Everyone is affected differently, most having a groggy time waking up and fully comprehending everything around them.

Jayne was the exception, and she asked Bubba again if he was okay. Now Bubba responded to her question.

"Ah, ha. Yeah, I'm okay." He felt like he had been hit with a sledgehammer to the head. Simple thoughts took much longer to answer than normal.

Jayne continued, "Captain Jones, we are in a security room. Let me do all the talking, and we always stay together! Do you understand?"

Bubba responded with a head shake up and down in approval.

The room had metal arms that extended from the ceiling. There were tracks every two feet with hydraulic arms just waiting for commands. They had six digits equally spaced at the end that formed their fingers, plus other joints that formed multiple elbows.

After 10 minutes, a hologram representing a metallic android appeared, speaking in English. It informed them to discard all weapons and go to the decontamination chamber. Bubba followed Jayne's lead as she placed her weapons on the table where they were standing. Jayne had five weapons, and Bubba had one.

Now, they walked to the chamber with Bubba waiting as Jayne entered the unit. After less than 2 seconds, Jayne came back out, grabbing Bubba's arm as she pulled him inside. The chamber was divided into three sections.

The sections were small, making it appear they were made for one person at a time. It was a 2- by 4-foot enclosure with a monitor on one of the short walls. On the opposite side of the monitor was a slot for discarded clothes.

Jayne had started taking her clothes off as Bubba turned to face the wall so as not to watch or see her nudity. She removed her panties, leaving her naked except for her necklace and ankle bracelets.

Now Jayne pulled Bubba around to see her, not being embarrassed, if anything a little annoyed.

She began, "Captain Jones, what are you waiting for? The quicker we get out of this security chamber, the safer we will be. I have put my life in your hands. Do you think I care that you see my body?"

Bubba finally realized she was not just a smart, beautiful woman, she was also a soldier, committed to the mission and her Captain. Now, she was helping Bubba undress. He used his key to remove the handcuffed briefcase attached to his wrist. Then he removed the rest of his clothes, putting them into the slot. Last, he reattached his handcuff to his left wrist with the briefcase in that hand.

Bubba, now in his own nudity, looked at Jayne with a facial expression that said, now what?

Jayne, looking at the monitor, said with authority, "Allow us to continue!"

The monitor flashed to life with a white screen, showing the words that were also spoken.

"Discard all accessories into the bin."

Jayne responded now with a touch of anger while still maintaining that she was in command.

"Scan all the accessories. They are not weapons! They are personal possessions and will not be discarded!"

In the moments that followed, Bubba was thinking to himself how strong and powerful Jayne was even when she was not in control. It reminded him of Brand. He wondered if he would ever get that way.

After what seemed like a long moment, the next door opened to a space the same size as the first section. This section was fitted with sprays of all different types and formulas. There was also a period where they put on eye protection while a very bright light saturated the room.

The entire experience was unpleasant, to put it nicely. Once it ended, the final door opened to the third room.

That room was filled with jumpsuits of all different sizes and in a few different styles. Also supplied were shoes of an ancient Japanese nature. Bubba would later say that he never felt cleaner in his life.

Once they were fully dressed, the door led to a hallway, which led to the main starship, which appeared in view. It seemed like the room was watching them.

As Bubba was walking through the hallway, he started to sense familiarity with the surroundings. Once they entered the starship, there was Dragonfly waiting for them. She was more beautiful than Bubba remembered. Her hair was longer but braided in three different styles, making her look 30 instead of her real age. She was a bit slimmer than the last time they were together. The garments she wore were made of gold and precious gems held together with fine silks and other fabrics.

Bubba remembered how she liked to make an entrance, and this did not disappoint.

"Dear, Bubba. It's wonderful to see you!" It was Dragonfly's true feelings when she said it. Then, her tone and manner changed a bit as she continued.

"Who is your friend?"

Now Jayne spoke, "I am not his friend. He is my Captain. You should address him as such!" There was no mistaking the irritation in her voice as she said it.

Dragonfly responded without anger, being more amused than upset, saying the following.

"Captain Jones, the room you occupied before is currently ready if you will accept it. There is a room next door for..." Dragonfly, who still did not know Jayne's name yet continued, "...I propose we meet in 2 hours to dine and hear about all of your adventures."

Before Bubba could reply, Jayne answered Dragonfly.

"My name is Jayne Stillwater. I will stay in the captain's room. We will see you in 2 hours. Thank you."

Then Bubba chimed in with, "I love that room." He had a big smile on his face, which changed the mood, and everyone replied with a smile of their own.

"And I am really hungry." Then, with a laugh, only Bubba had entered the surroundings.

9

DOUBLE CROSS

Utago was moving through space at a speed that could only be described the way a baby crawls in the dark. That darkness was everywhere and completely encompassing. If that were not bad enough, he was very alone. That area of space is seldom used with the thought of just getting lucky, far from reality.

Because of the time crystal, food would eventually be his downfall. It had been days that turned into weeks. Then, the weeks started to add up. With that much time alone, true introspection began.

He was pleased with the recent decisions made. Making sure Bubba and Jayne survived the killer computer virus found on the distressed ship. It would have been easy to try and save himself at all costs.

What good is fame if you have to lose all your honor in getting it? His thoughts drifted through his life, one moment in childhood the next 60 years later. The society he left hailed conformity as a prized virtue. Knowing he was different from such an early age, living in a community so intense on everyone thinking the same feelings and thoughts.

Leaving that world was easy for him, while his friends and family thought he was crazy, hoping he would return quickly to finally see the path to freedom. That was how his people viewed their lack of choices, as the path to real freedom.

His thoughts went to what started his passion for exploring. His father was a cave explorer, there being many caves on his home world. About 70 had not been explored. They were considered too dangerous and were restricted to enter, for reasons not stated.

Utago's father was a very brave man who would be labeled a non-conformist in most worlds. Father and son would often explore the restricted caves figuring their expertise was sufficient to the task. In those dark caves where he never knew what he would find, hoping it would be some type of treasure, his love for exploring began. The excitement of just being where he was not supposed to be, plus the great unknown, solidified his plans to explore. Unlike being in the caves, where no one could know about his adventures, he wanted to be well known in the galaxy for his bravery and accomplishments.

Utago was glad to have made the choices that were his to make, even now, facing death, which was coming, and the choices that had taken him here. Yet he would make no different decisions to avoid this outcome. That feeling brought him a form of peace.

Then a smile came to his face, remembering something Bubba had said. Bubba was recalling times in his past after he had met Brand. How, when not in his presence, he would think to himself in hard situations? What would Brand do?

Utago started to think exactly what his hero would do. Then, a bigger smile came to his face. In the short time he had known Brand, he seemed to do everything that would get himself killed. Exactly as Utago had now done. There was a funny irony in it all. He wanted to be like Brand. Unfortunately, Brand never seemed to care about his own death.

Most would have given up. If not, they would have definitely gone mad. Isolation brings madness to the door of each of us. It is a rare being that can resist opening it.

Math runs the universe with probabilities being its odds maker. No matter how small a chance may exist, math demands that sometimes, be it immensely rare, it will happen.

Imagine the furthest odds against something just by the way it is defined. One in, yet that one means it can happen. No matter how small that one chance may be.

————

Jayne did not trust Dragonfly, and there were very few she trusted. Bubba had earned her loyalty to their mission. Yet, really trusting him, especially with his poor decision-making and naivety in most things, showed her commitment to the task at hand.

"Captain, we must be on our guard at all times now. This is her ship, and we are currently her prisoners. Do not reveal any information regarding our plans."

Some would be offended or consider that insubordination of their power. Bubba did not belong to that group and replied.

"Thank you, Jayne, I'll do my best." He said it with a serious face and tone to his voice.

Bubba then added, "Jayne, there will come a time when I will need you to totally trust my judgment, ok?"

Jayne now looked a bit confused. "Of course, Captain."

He was feeling better as time proceeded along. The fog of thought and lack of body control dissipated. Bubba really did not know what to expect with Dragonfly's intervention. A part of him said maybe she would get us to the Nevermore, and my role would be concluded. Of course, the other part said she would take the prize, and at best, we would live to tell the tale.

This reminded him of listening and questioning Brand while he told his tales.

He could hear Brand saying, "Once you're halfway through the adventure, most of your choices are limited. You just make do with what you have left."

They really did not have a choice not to dine with Dragonfly. Nor did they have control over where her starship would take them from here. Even with those thoughts, Bubba was in good spirits that they would complete the journey and give Brand the secret cure.

Bubba knew his way to the private yet very grand dinner room. There was a large, beautiful dining hall within the great starship. The smaller one felt even more elegant, being that it only seated 12 guests.

It had a long rectangular table that looked like pink marble. Dragonfly, who had not yet arrived, her seat being at the head of one end of the table. Bubba and Jayne were seated two seats down from Dragonfly's seat and across from each other.

Jayne, who already did not like the fact that they were not sitting next to each other, grudgingly went to her designated chair. There were fancy name displays where each person was to sit.

Once they were seated, and after about 5 minutes, Dragonfly appeared in a kimono dress. It was red and black in style with a matching hat. Once she was seated, there were 6 people in the room performing all serving duties. That included pulling the chair out for her and moving it to its final destination.

Dragonfly started the conversation by saying, "I want to hear every detail concerning your adventures, but before you begin, I have to ask, what happened to Utago?"

Instantly, the mood became somber. Both Bubba and Jayne's memory of their friend and savior flooded their minds. Bubba felt guilty regarding his death, which until that moment he had not registered was his fault. Now he had the title of Captain, and Utago, whom he should have protected, died saving him.

Jayne, who could clearly see the distress it was bringing her Captain, said.

"He gave his life to save Captain Jones and myself. He died with honor."

Now, Bubba, who was still at a loss with words, looked like he wanted to add something, yet he was saying nothing."

From that moment until they were done relating the entire story, Dragonfly said nothing.

She already knew about the Jinn and most of their struggles until she found them. She thought how it was always interesting to see how honest someone will be, especially when you are going to trick them.

Once everyone had finished their meals and as they were waiting for dessert to be served, Dragonfly started to speak.

"Captain Jones, I have always treated you not only with respect but as a personal friend. When you visited me on Mars, did I not offer you the elixir of extended life?"

Bubba responded in his serious mode, "You sure did."

Dragonfly resumed, "Taking you to safety from the attack on Mars and then giving you my personal starship to see Brand and the General fight, did I ever ask for anything in return? Any favor or price for my kindness bestowed on you?"

Bubba, looking right into Dragonfly's eyes, said, "But you are going to ask now, right?" He said it with a power of knowledge, almost like he was baiting her.

"Captain, this is a win-win situation. You lend me the Jinn for my one wish, and I will give it back to you while also taking you to the Nevermore. We both win." Dragonfly finished that speech with one of her most beautiful smiles.

Bubba had not taken his eyes off Dragonfly, "If I refuse?"

No words were spoken by Dragonfly. Her words were actions. Maybe she was using some form of mental telepathy. In the next instant, the two servers on each side of the table now had some form of gun pointed at Bubba and Jayne. It was done fast, and all four servers performed their actions simultaneously in drawing their guns and aiming them at Jayne and Bubba.

Bubba, who still was looking at Dragonfly, started anew, "It won't work for you unless you know how to call the Jinn. Also, there are rules to making your wish work correctly." He had more to say, but Dragonfly interrupted him.

She had a smile like you would look at a child who you are going to correct.

"Bubba Jones, you are not Brand Wright. That bluff is something he would try, and he was always just lucky. Do you really think I need you to operate it? I could kill you right now and take it if I want to. Yet

I don't desire to do that. So please, Captain, make the smart decision. That is what good captains do."

Bubba, to his credit, was unshaken by all that was happening. Almost as if he expected it and preparations were already made for its presence.

Bubba was now ready for his time, "You're the second person to tell me that, it did not go well for the first."

That was said with a smile as if he were laughing inside himself.

"I accept your offer on one condition, we go to LaTaFree. I have a contact there who will pick Jayne up and take her back there."

Now Jayne interrupted Bubba with anger, shouting, "Captain, what are you doing!?"

For the first time, Dragonfly and Jayne, plus whoever else was in that room, saw Bubba mad. He now put his full gaze on Jayne and with a scream that shocked everyone there.

"Soldier, shut up! Not another word out of you! That is an order!"

No one spoke a word. He had intimidated everyone there with the suddenness, with the forcefulness, in his words.

Bubba again spoke, now looking at Dragonfly. "When I started this mission, besides helping Brand, I made a promise to try and make sure people would not die. On Earth, eight people died, and then Utago died in saving Jayne and me. Whether Brand gets saved or not, I will not have another person's death on my watch. I understand now why Brand did not want us to do any of this. He would not want any more deaths. This must end. Once Jayne is safe on the planet, I will give you the Jinn plus how to call it. Also, the rules if you like."

Dragonfly was in thought. She said nothing, just looking at Bubba. Then, after what felt like a long time, she responded.

"It will take two days to get there, one if we push it. You're right about Brand. He had lost his taste for killing. Truth is, so have I. Once we drop Jayne off at LaTaFree, we will finish this mission together."

Then she added, "Captain, I suggest Jayne be detained in a cabin until we arrive at our destination."

Bubba now was a different person, "Agreed, make it one day."

Jayne was in shock. Of course, there still were guns on Bubba and her. More than that, it was the way Bubba had just addressed her, the way they were all talking around her like she wasn't in the room.

Jayne then spoke with an ominous voice, "Captain Jones, I will kill you. No matter how long it takes."

Dragonfly then spoke to the servers behind Jayne, "Please take Jayne Stillwater to the pink room."

Bubba's thoughts were not on Jayne or the guns behind him. They were not on Dragonfly either. His thoughts were on his friend Brand, feeling that he finally understood why Brand wanted no more adventures, no missions, just isolation.

It was a whirlwind of knowledge, and in that instant, so much became apparent. It was clarity. Even if he never saw Brand again, he now understood so much more.

Bubba then said, "I will be in my room. Contact me when we arrive at LaTaFree."

The next day, they were in orbit around the planet. Bubba had not left his room and was informed they were there. He went to the command center and contacted his friend, who was a high official on LaTaFree. An arrangement was made. Jayne would be picked up and brought back to him.

Bubba had met him when Brand's fight with the general brought them there. Some people you have an instant connection with, as was the case with their friendship. He told Bubba that if you ever needed anything, no matter what, just contact him. At the time, Bubba thought that would never happen.

While Bubba was talking to him from the ship, he said, "She will not be happy with me. Hopefully, one day, she will understand. I cannot thank you enough and will not be able to repay this favor."

Jayne was not released from her room until all was set. The transport ship had arrived, and Jayne was led to it with the help of Dragonfly's crew. Bubba did not want to be there. It was killing him not being able to say goodbye and thank her for all she had done. There was no room for any slip-ups. It would be safer to forego the goodbye.

It all happened without incident, a great anti-climactic ending. Once she was gone, it felt like everything was different. A great loneliness overtook his spirit, a sadness that he had rarely felt. The last time was when Brand was thought dead from the shrinking pyramid in Antarctica.

In a way, he could be bolder, as the only life in jeopardy was now his own. Dragonfly had called him to meet her in the ship's study. That room was very relaxing and had a mix of a library plus plant heaven in a retro-style setting.

Dragonfly was in extremely good spirits, for she could not stop smiling. She was seated behind a large table. There were two chairs in front which Bubba sat on one. They were both identical and nice but not as nice as Dragonfly's chair.

Bubba now realized that Dragonfly always made it a point to let everyone know she was in charge, more deserving than the rest, and getting the best in everything.

He removed the handcuff that had become part of his left wrist. It almost felt unnatural not having it attached to himself. He unlocked the briefcase and put it on the table, pushing it to Dragonfly.

Then he began talking, which at first Dragonfly paid no attention to. This is what Bubba was saying.

"I asked Brand how he beat people that were much smarter than himself. He said they were the easiest to beat and left it at that. He would always need prodding to find out what he was really saying. So, I kept on him, and after the third push, he said, because they think they are the smartest in the room. Again, I prodded him, asking how that makes it easy." Now Bubba saw that he had Dragonfly's full attention.

She was looking at him with a look like it was the first time she had seen him. It was a mean stare.

Bubba continued, "Brand said that's because they think they are so smart that nobody could out-think them. They are less paranoid than others, where someone less confident in their mental abilities tends to check more things." Then he paused to make his last point.

"You and I both know Brand was the king of double-cross."

With that, Bubba stopped talking and now had the smile Dragonfly had started with. For the first time during what he referred to in his mind as "Bubba's Time," which was his adventures to save Brand, he felt really good. He had beat Dragonfly, at least for now, and that was a big thing, even bigger. He probably saved Jayne's life. In his mind, he had done good.

Dragonfly had the look of someone who had just realized a truth they had never known before.

"I should kill you right now. A year ago, I would have done it without a thought. You're just a human, weak and stupid. It always bothered me how Brand would get the better of my encounters with him. How do you know that I would not make my wish and give it back to you? Why would you assume I would cheat you?"

Bubba, unaffected by her threat of death, responded, now more relaxed and with a bigger smile.

"Because one of the rules is to be very careful who you give the Jinn to once you have made your wish. You would be one of the worst to give it to. Once you have made your wish, you will figure out a way to get someone else to make a wish for you. Maybe to fix your first wish. Then, you would keep using people to make wishes for you, so you would get unlimited wishes. I can see your thinking. Why do I think this? Because that is the way you are." Then, as an afterthought, he added.

"Why would you care about Jayne, Brand, or me?"

Dragonfly now looked different, not happy nor angry. The look would have to be described as sad. She had her head slightly bowed.

She said the following, "I don't care about Jayne, but Utago, Brand, and you are the only people I did like. Now Utago and Brand are dead. Neither were human, which was appealing. They reminded me of myself. You were the one human I liked.

Then her mood changed instantly, she seemed to become a different person, and spoke.

"I want to form an alliance. We work together, shadow Jayne from a distance, eventually returning to the Nevermore to get our friend back."

Then she added, "Captain, I underestimated you. The fact that you got the better of me impresses me. Truth is, I am lonely and enjoy your company. I promise to sometime in the future get you back to Earth." Now, she was smiling with that smile only Dragonfly had.

10

JAYNE STILLWATER

The pilot of Jayne's transport to LaTaFree was a jovial person. His talking only annoyed Jayne, not mentioning all his questions directed to her. They were in the form of how are you feeling? Do you know Gentry Lord? Have you been staying in LaTaFree for a long time? It seemed there was no end to it. He had given Jayne a language translator that looked like a headband. It worked by inputting the speech spoken and then translating it directly into her head. It was standard for galactic translation and worked flawlessly.

Jayne made no comments which only had her pilot answer all his questions to her in his own references. She was hurt, feeling betrayed, and belittled by the way Captain Jones had just treated her. Her thoughts went to more and more questions. How could he feel that she would not be helpful in completing the mission? How could he trust Dragonfly to give the Jinn back? And even more importantly, what should she do now?

The planet LaTaFree was an exotic vacation playground for their galaxy, accommodating all varieties of entertainment. There were the arenas that held fights to the death while also having the most beautiful gardens and sceneries ever experienced. Something for everyone was the motto of the land.

Their security force was very well-trained, extremely professional, and almost invisible to the average tourist. With so many different types of races together, there was no room for weakness in maintaining order.

Gentry Lord was the head of that security. He had met Bubba Jones during the fight between Brand Wright, aka Plutoneus, and General Max. Even for LaTaFree, it was the main show gathering the who's-who of the galaxy.

There are some people that as soon as you meet them, there becomes a strong bond of friendship. That is what happened when Bubba and Gentry met. Like long-lost brothers, their bond was quick and strong.

Gentry was rich by anyone's measure. The man had everything, including a great job, wife, and family. Multiple homes and transports plus a wide collection of unique one-of-a-kind objects.

Loving adventures, he was happy to accommodate his friend's request. Not knowing what to expect from Jayne, he had his servants prepare all types of food, music, and art for her arrival.

That was the way things were done on LaTaFree, trying to make any event as big and pleasurable as possible. LaTaFree was a combination of many different worlds yet still maintained its own identity. One of those features is to try to make everything spectacular.

Jayne was hurt, not physically but worse, so her meeting with Gentry Lord did not impress her. She would be trusting no one from this point on.

He was an older man looking in his sixties, well-dressed and spoken, yet anyone as rich as he was could never be trusted. Jayne's primary nature was being a soldier. From her earliest memories, it was her duty to a larger cause. Collecting money was just greedy and self-serving.

Gentry kept going on about how wonderful Bubba was until Jayne could no longer take it. Looking Gentry in his eyes, she spoke the following with attitude.

"Just so you understand clearly, I wish Captain Jones were dead!"

Right after, she said that everything changed. There was a blue mist coming from her chest. It was pouring out, getting thicker and becoming solid in front of her. She could see Gentry, who was frozen, the form in front of her now becoming a real person.

The Jinn became a handsome man in his early thirties, with black hair, blue eyes, and an olive complexion. Now complete in shape and substance, it looked at Jayne and spoke.

"Mistress, is that your wish?"

"No." Was said quickly and quietly. As if now afraid to speak out loud, Jayne almost whispered, "Where did you come from?" As she asked the question, her mind raced with facts, adding to her confusion.

"My last master changed my container and then gave it to you."

Jayne thought, *that's why Bubba was in his home on Earth for so long. Then, on the ship, he gave Utago the book and me the watch.* Her mind remembered how he asked her to keep it with her at all times.

Her thoughts went to poor Captain Jones. He was so far ahead of everyone, and he gave his life to keep the mission going. The briefcase was just a distraction, but he played it perfectly.

Then she started to feel awful about how she treated him and what she said about killing him. She was brought out of thought by the Jinn's next statement.

"Call me my mistress when you are ready with your wish."

Jayne had another question.

"Did your last master make a wish?"

Now, the Jinn seemed to become more awake.

"No, he did not, which is quite unusual. Very few pass on their wish."

Jayne then told the Jinn she would contact him with her wish when she was ready.

The Jinn disappeared quicker than the time it had taken to appear. Then, time started again, and Gentry was talking about Captain Jones. He responded to her outburst with the following.

"Well, he cares about you, and you are luckier for it. You should show gratitude."

Jayne, who now was a different person than a moment before, answered Gentry.

"You are right, sir. May I please spend some time alone to rest?"

Gentry seemed confused, like he realized something had happened, yet he had no idea what that something was. In his mind, he also wanted time to figure out what just occurred.

"Of course, there is a room set up just for you and your needs. Please enjoy as much time as needed." With that and some commands yelled to his servants, Jayne was led to her new prison.

————

Initially, Sam Smith wanted to go alone, just him and a pilot flying to LaTaFree. His power and position made that impossible. Being too important can work against oneself, this being the case. Even if he demanded to go alone, he knew he would be shadowed. Fighting that type of thing is fruitless, so silent acquiescence was the only recourse.

Then it was to be him plus 15 soldiers on a medium-sized craft, which now turned into the following.

One battleship with hundreds of soldiers plus Sam Smith and Adam Knight. The ship was one of the secret space fleet's finest, having just recently been activated. The trip was not long, with two days getting them there at a leisurely pace.

They had already contacted the Governor of LaTaFree, who wanted to greet them personally. The greater the attention Sam received, the more unhappy he became. He had no real purpose in going there. He felt he would look silly with nothing really there to accomplish.

His initial plan was to try to relive the feelings Brand Wright had felt there. Walk the same roads and enter the exact buildings Brand had done.

Sam would never acknowledge that after dealing with Brand, he had changed. Maybe it was that fact that intrigued him so much. At this point, he felt he knew more about Brand than Bolt. Brand was more than just his reality-bending abilities. More than just having greater luck than what is normal, he changes the people around him.

Sam always thought deeply and started to confirm his belief with the names that would prove to be evidence of his new theory.

Bubba was a perfect example. He was just a person with an interest in esoteric things but never really got involved in the action. That all changed once Brand's contact happened in his life. There were many more examples, with Sam being one of them.

Sam spent much of his time on the journey with Adam as if he were studying him, mostly asking opinionated questions and just listening to Adam's answers. To Sam, Adam was a very peaceful being who was always trying to appease those around him. Avoiding conflict where most would not. Adam never complained about anything. On the contrary, he was very grateful for everything that came his way.

That was so different than how Sam saw things. He had earned his status and expected nothing but the finest accouterments in life.

Tomorrow, they will reach their destination and will be walking on LaTaFree.

It could best be described as a mixture of everything: old and new constructions, foreign and familiar buildings that lined the roads. They led to great plazas that were filled with the smell of all types of foods. Sounds coming from everywhere and all sides. Some people pitch their products while others play music. Then, there were the performers that seemed to be around each corner.

LaTaFree had a feel of so many different things. One of their mottos, as they had many, was, "Something for everyone!"

Sam and Adam, in the center of a group of warriors, 18 to be exact, were walking to one of the main plazas within LaTaFree. It held their biggest arena, where Brand and the General had their death match.

Sam was glad he had made the trip. No video or virtual reality headset would really do it justice. That was the point of the trip, to actually smell, taste, and hear, to really feel the experience. And what was to come next could never be experienced without being there.

There were great homes set back from the path that had their space defined by walls. Each home was different and had a unique wall defining its space.

Adam was fixated on one of the mansions that had a castle appearance. It had two towers standing guard at each end of the front of the fortress, with stone walls that ran from the ground to its highest heights. Midway from the towers were banners in gold and purple that ran to the top of a lower building closer to the stone wall in a stonework design similar to its larger version. Then there was the yard in front, which had to be at least half a mile before its wall started.

The wall was made of stone with vertical open spaces that were four feet in height and three inches in width for every four feet. Thus, providing protection while also allowing the defenders a chance to engage the attacker.

The gate was a large metal fixture that had a heavy, strong look, and it was the only entry point past the wall. There was a guard house located on either side of the gate, giving the entire appearance a very formidable look.

Adam, turning to Sam, said, "We need to get inside there right now!"

To most, they would have questioned Adam, why, what was going to happen, and things of that nature. Sam was never like most people. He was always different, which had served him well, at least in his mind.

Sam still had not answered Adam, and now the Governor of LaTaFree shouted to get their attention. He moved quickly toward their entourage with a warm greeting to Sam.

"Dear friend, welcome to LaTaFree. It is a pleasure and honor to have you visit our home. Is there anything I can do to make your stay here more pleasurable?"

Sam's nature was to be aloof and, with almost no expression, said the following.

"I would like to visit that home right now, please, if that is not too much trouble." His tone at the end was almost a challenge as he pointed to the spot that Adam was interested in.

Then Sam added in a gentle voice, "Thank you."

The governor was still looking at them, yet you could see he was really not there. His eyes had a blank stare. It was assumed that he had some implant that was connected to their home world, and after about twenty seconds, he was fully back with them.

"Mr. Sam Smith, sir, that will not be a problem. It is a beautiful home, and the owner is also the head of our security. I have contacted him, and he is delighted to make your acquaintance.

Once they had passed the gate, Adam separated from the group and headed towards the small building. Most eyes were on his movement and the direction he was headed. One of the soldiers looked at Sam, who motioned him with his head moving up and down to go after him. Within a few seconds, 14 soldiers were running behind Adam, trying to catch up.

Sam trained himself to look at things others did not notice. It was then that his eyes traveled past where Adam was running towards the entire structure in front of them. It was small, but there was definitely movement on the top of the right tower.

11

FINDING AN EXIT

Jayne still had her weapons, yet she was in a fortress loaded with guards. The areas that looked promising for escape each held problems in that regard. The first obstacles were the doors that led to the outside. Each had guards on both sides, and the physical release mechanism came from a different location. Even if the guards on both sides could have been killed, there was still the problem of unlocking the door.

All the guards had weapons, and all exits were guarded. Then, of course, there were the cameras. So many that all moves were monitored. Anything she inspected was noted by the electronic eyes of the home.

They were very nice to her and seemed to want to accommodate her desires, except for leaving. Some might not have minded that much. It was a very nice prison. Jayne would never accept it, so she kept observing and trying to figure out an escape.

On her second day there, after meeting Gentry Lord, she was summoned to his study.

He was interrogating her about something that he had no real knowledge of. Jayne was no fool and quickly realized he was fishing for something he knew nothing about. She figured that if he did know, he would have physically just taken it, with her being alive or dead having no consequence.

That was her advantage, keeping her secret. Jayne was tempted to use the Jinn to escape this confinement. Its purpose was for her hero, and she would not use it for her own wants or needs. She had the power of focus and love for her mission. Power and love can be very hard to beat, even when being a prisoner in an inescapable place.

Gentry started by asking, "Did you sleep well? Is there anything I can do to make your stay more pleasurable?"

Jayne tried the subtle approach, "I would like a tour outside your home to enjoy the town."

Gentry answered, "Currently, it is not safe for you to venture from my home. There is a courtyard for you to enjoy the outdoors. When we first met yesterday, I reviewed our encounter. As you are aware, there were many cameras and something strange occurred during our meeting. I would like your help in understanding what happened."

Jayne looked innocent, "Well, I will try my best."

Gentry, uncomfortable in his current ignorance, began, "Well, at one point during our meeting, I seemed to have been frozen while you were talking about something the cameras did not see. It lasted less than two minutes, so it can't be a glitch in the recording. What exactly happened during that time?"

Now Jayne, acting like he was mad, and replied, "I don't remember that!"

This only upset Gentry, who was used to servants and underlings around him who were complying with his every demand. Now, he forced Jayne to watch the recording, implying that after that, there could be no denying that something did happen.

Jayne politely watched the episode displayed in front of her eyes. Everything was there but the sight of the Jinn and the smoke he appeared from. Also, the sound had cut off as soon as the blue smoke emanated from the watch hanging from Jayne's chest.

"Maybe someone has invaded your technology, a virus or something like that. I have no memory of the event you have recorded." For some reason, the thought that Gentry would soon resort to torture to get answers entered her mind. She must escape this prison quickly, or everything will be lost.

The next two days, she surveyed the entire building, finding maybe one possible way out. She would make her move in the morning, being that daylight would be needed. Her mind felt that time was of the essence, always in constant fear her secret would be revealed.

A part of her mind was surprised by Gentry's laid-back approach to what had happened. Then, her rational side explained that if he had any idea how important the event was, he would be all over it. She surmised that it was just an oddity, a peculiarity, something that he would later resolve when he decided the time was right. She was his prisoner, and to his mentality, he had all the time in the world to elucidate the issue.

There were two towers that sprang up on each side of the great home, each having a completely open view of everything below. They were barely guarded, given their height, and the best someone would be able to do was reach the top. They were at least four stories high. Once at the top, where could they go? The only recourse would be to descend back to where they started.

One guard protected the stairs leading to that high perch. Of course, there were cameras everywhere about. Once she made her move, there would be no going back.

She had seen there were banners leading from the towers to a lower portion of a roof below. It was too hard to judge exactly how far below the banners started from the top of the towers. Jayne figured that would be found out once she got there.

The plan was to jump onto the banners and work her way to the ground. Then, taking any road going away from that prison. She knew her chances were slim. There were no other options. If she remained, it would only be a matter of time before her secret would be discovered.

In the back of her mind, she thought as long as she held the Jinn, there would always be a chance. Deep down, she was so proud of Captain Jones. He had the Jinn and never used it. Not only that, but he gave it away, showing how truly committed he was to the mission.

Before this moment, she had always felt stronger than Bubba, in both mind and body. Now she realized how truly great he was while fearing she would not meet the moment. She thought to herself, *there comes a time when even the slimmest chance is worth taking when each of us has to go beyond our limits.*

She knew she was taking a leap of faith both spiritually and physically. She thought about how this might be the end of her life. How grateful she was for what she was given. Most would say it was a hard life, but that is not how she felt. People always commented on her bravery, yet it did not seem to her she was being brave. She was just being herself.

Jayne was now getting into the mindset of what would come next. She did not want to kill anyone, especially the guards holding her prisoner. To her, they were only following orders, as she would do.

The fact is, even if the guards did not kill her, they would do nothing to stop it from being done.

This was the game they played called life. Win if you can but survive at all costs. She was hoping she could lure him into the stairway leading up the tower. It was a spiral rising clockwise, just like the ancient castles on Earth.

If she could get above the guard on the staircase, she would have an advantage, though it would be a slight one. Most of her escape plan was not really thought out.

Bravery and stupidity can be hard to define. Most escape plans demand taking chances. The fact that you are imprisoned means your prior plans have already failed. They were made when you have plenty of time to think things through.

Any prisoner of war who has escaped readily admits that most, if not a big part, was luck in making it happen.

The guard standing in front of the tower's entrance was old. Of course, that is relative. His age was somewhere around fifty. In his profession, that was a bit past your prime, at least physically, which Jayne was counting on.

On the other hand, older people had more experience, an advantage. The fact that they have survived in a dangerous profession is its own statement.

Jayne had many talents. She could be soft and gentle, and she was sweet with words and actions. It would surprise people who did not know her. The side most saw was hard, like a shield always protecting her. She would let her feelings be known when it mattered, regardless of who the people were or the consequences that might follow.

She approached the guard and asked, "Why do they have you here guarding this tower. There is no escape at the top." She said it in an innocent manner, acting truly curious about the subject.

The guard looked at her for what seemed to be a long time before responding.

"Gentry Lord is excessive concerning security. I imagine he is more concerned with someone entering from the top."

Jayne then moved closer to the old guard and asked, "Do you think I am pretty?" Again, with that innocent tone.

"You're very pretty."

Now, Jayne was going to make her move, and she moved even closer to the guard. They were only an inch apart from each other.

Jayne, speaking in a soft tone while blinking her eyes more than what was natural, said, "It's been a long time since I have felt a man's touch. What do you say?"

The old guard started breathing heavier and said, "I get off in two hours..."

"No, I am in the mood now!" And with that, Jayne cupped the back of his hand, moving it until it touched her left breast.

Then, moving his hand while looking into his eyes, she said, "Let's go into the tower, a few steps up. It will make it more exciting."

It was obvious the guard led a lonely life by how excited he had become.

Looking deeply into Jayne's eyes, "No tricks."

"Where am I going to go?" Was Jayne's response in a bewildered look.

They both entered the tower, ascending the stairs. After reaching the tenth step, the guard told Jayne to stop. They were well out of sight from the entranceway, where they had started. Still, very far from reaching the top, the guard said the following while he pulled out his gun.

"Now I will have my weapon out the whole time, so don't try any tricks. Give me your weapons. Yes, I know you have more than one."

Jayne had figured she would be weaponless during this event. It would have been far too easy to just pull out her weapon, set it to stun, shoot, and move on. Yet that also involved risks, as her plan relied on stealth.

She remembered CW showing up one day during combat training on the Nevermore. He had told them, "Your best weapon during any combat is your mind. Never rely on what gun you are holding or who is next to you. Your mind will keep you alive."

She gave the guard all her weapons, two guns, and two knives, plus what also looked like brass knuckles. Her thoughts were that the more relaxed he became, the easier it would be to defeat him.

Next, she removed her sweater. She was not wearing anything underneath it. Jayne was always amazed at how shy people were about nudity. She had a firm, muscular body with less gravity pulling on it, being most of her time was on the Nevermore.

The guard had frozen just looking at her breasts. His right hand held a gun, while his left hand was free of any burdens.

Jayne then started to unbuckle his belt while also unzipping his pants. She pulled it down to his knees, which was on purpose, hoping it would entangle him when she made her move.

She then pushed him to sit down, saying, "Relax, I am not going to bite." Looking at his face, they made eye contact, and she gave him a sweet smile.

It was imperative that he not be tense when she would attack. Jayne moved in closer, her breasts pushing against his groin. She could feel his body relaxing now that he was sitting and leaning back, with her chest in his private area.

With a cat-like movement, Jayne pushed her way up to his face, stopping at his neck. Then, slowly, taking both his arms with each of her hands, pushing them above his head.

"I like to kiss." With that, she started kissing his neck. They were slow kisses, like if you had something that was extremely valuable, and your kisses were how much you treasured it.

Her entire body was on top of his, with each part of her glued to his skin except for one leg. The guard was now truly relaxing, his defenses at the lowest levels since she started talking to him. In her mind, the time was now.

With one leg that was not touching his body, she drew it up and back. Ramming it forward with her knee, trying to hit his testicles, knowing that she would have one chance to get it right.

The ability to surprise your enemy and bring great pain instantly is a strong weapon. The fact that your opponent may outweigh you or have superior strength can always be compromised with strategy.

Her aim was almost perfect, and the plan was then to put all her attention to the gun in his right hand.

The guard's reaction was so severe he threw Jayne off his body with her landing against the inside wall of the staircase. She also hit her shoulder, elbow, and leg on the stairs yet felt no pain, just adrenaline.

She moved behind the guard, who was now bent over holding his groin area. He still had his gun in his right hand. She was going to disable it but then saw her own gun sitting right in front of her. Picking it up, setting it to stun, Jayne fired one burst.

His body then froze up while at the same time tumbling down the stairs. Jayne quickly put her sweater on, secured all her weapons, and headed up the tower.

It was then that the pain started to filter in. Like a bomb, all areas affected shouted their discomfort to her brain. Her head had a cut that was bleeding well. Her shoulder and elbow plus knee were also tightening up and hurting.

The staircase seemed to never end. Around and around, she stumbled to the top. Her excitement to possibly escape her current situation pushed her past what a normal person could do or withstand.

Finally, she stepped into the open air. The air at the top of the tower tasted fresher, cleaner than the courtyard air. It was a feeling like having cabin fever and finally, after way too long in confinement, tasting the outside world again.

Quickly, she looked over the entire scene below her. From her height, she could see way past the wall. She was looking for large groups that she could become lost in.

It appeared there was a man running in the direction she would eventually be in. There was no time to wait. Again, she thought about using the Jinn.

In her mind, she could use it to escape and be back on the Nevermore, and then someone else could use it to wish CW back. The problem was that as long as she possessed it without using it, she could still control the final event. Once used, it would have to be trusted by someone else. Having the power of a Jinn can be too great a temptation for most.

No, she would try to escape and let fate do what it will. Instead of trying to grab the banner with her fingers, she would use her arms and pull it towards her once it was under her control.

Like a bodybuilder flexing, she moved her arms into that position and stepped up to the edge of the tower. The banner looked tiny below her, being at least 25 feet from her view.

Her body was now hurting, but the blood had stopped flowing from her head. For a moment, she thought about how much her life had changed since she left the Nevermore. Then, without another thought, she pushed off the wall, eyes wide open, plunging towards a banner that was the only thing that mattered in her life.

It amazed her how fast the moment came. She headed right for it, catching the banner with her left arm and then instantly moving her right arm to secure her left to her body. It all happened so fast yet worked exactly how she had planned it in her mind.

Then, two seconds later, everything changed again. The banner's attachment to the tower dislodged due to the weight and sudden impact of Jayne's arrival on it. Now, she was swinging towards the only wall it remained attached to.

She was moving fast when the man running her way stopped in the perfect spot to break her momentum and fall from the banner.

Jayne felt bad about hitting him, but there was no way around him except to let go earlier than what would be prudent. With her feet banging into Adam, sending him straight to the ground, Jayne slowed down and landed on the ground, not any worse than she had started from the tower.

Adam still had not moved from the initial collision with Jayne. Her instinct was to run to the wall and escape.

Jayne would not be able to verbalize to herself, but she had changed once she found out about Bubba's plan. Being deceptive was extremely important, yet it was more than that. Sometimes, you have to go against reason to do things that seem to be counterproductive.

Before she had started this mission with Bubba and Utago, without any hesitation, she would have been heading for the wall. Jayne wasn't that person anymore.

She ran over to Adam, who was still face down on the ground.

Speaking in an excited but gentle tone, "Hey, are you okay?"

She waited to hope he would move or say something. Then, like someone coming up for air out of water, he responded in pain.

"Oh, I'm good." Which was apparently the opposite of how he really felt.

"Thank you. I got to go!" As soon as Jayne said that, two doors opened at different spots from the castle, and the guards rushed towards them.

Luckily for Adam and Jayne, the 14 soldiers had also arrived at their location at that moment. The soldiers quickly broke into two groups, with 8 soldiers guarding Adam and Jayne while the six others spread out their positions to guard the first group.

There became two lines with an ominous silence, just weapons facing weapons. The guards had formed a V-shaped formation, with the soldiers forming a tank around Adam and Jayne while their other members were spread apart in an open position.

It all happened so fast that the Governor still had not responded but was going back into a blank stare. Sam Smith watched and said nothing.

There was an electricity in the air, the feeling that at any moment, all weapons would be fired. It is hard to say how long that lasted. It felt like a long moment to the people involved, but maybe it was only one or two seconds.

Also, what exactly set everything off is still in question. Maybe it was a firecracker or just a twig on the ground that made a loud noise once stepped on. There was definitely a sound, yet where it actually came from is unknown to all involved.

The first two shots seemed to happen almost simultaneously, each with a different sound, and then a war of sounds followed. Each side lost half their people after the first rounds went off.

The soldiers and guards that remained now were taking better advantage of the landscape and protection afforded by it. The tank group containing Jayne and Adam rushed towards the wall, away from the action, with the soldiers at the rear-firing their weapons, providing cover during the escape.

Then, two big ships that used anti-gravity propulsion arrived on the scene. They each had three big guns situated on the bottom. Two were located midway the length of the entire craft, while the third was just under the front.

From one of the ships came a thunderous sound with the words, "Everyone drop your weapons and disengage now!" The sound was loud, yet there was something else inside it. The feeling that compliance was mandatory, not out of pain but a genuine desire to want to comply.

Now, many things were happening at once. Gentry Lord approached the Governor and Sam Smith while more guards from his home entered the fray. At the same time, android security guards approached the soldiers and guards.

If that was not enough action, medical personnel arrived, going straight to the injured who were being separated from the dead. As fast as the conflict began, it was over quickly, leaving the people in charge to sort it all out.

There was a private conversation between the Governor and Gentry Lord. They each had chips installed in their brains. This gave them a form of telepathic communication.

The Governor began, "What is going on? These Earthlings are backed by some powerful races. Since Plutoneus fight with the General, they are known for being fierce fighters who battle to the death. They are a large group of potential customers. Who is the woman escaping your home?"

Gentry Lord replied in his mind, "Bubba Jones, Plutoneus best friend, sent Jayne, that woman, to me. She is hiding some great secret, something I can tell is very powerful. I was just about to reveal that secret. We need to keep her here!"

The Governor of LaTaFree had a strange look he was giving Gentry Lord, his position being higher than Gentry. All he replied was, "You're making a big mistake."

Gentry Lord glared back at him with, "You're making a bigger mistake!" Then he turned to Sam Smith, who had not moved or said a word to anyone.

Gentry Lord began, "My great apologies to your people who have been killed or hurt. This is a misunderstanding. Once my guest returns to my home, everything will be made right."

Sam Smith was always a man of few words.

"No, we will *all* be leaving now."

The Governor now spoke, "Of course, if she wants to leave, that is her choice. Please let me make things right. We will make reparations for your losses. Please allow me to show you all that our planet LaTaFree has to offer at no charge."

Sam Smith just looked at both men and said, "Thank you, but we are leaving now." With that, he whispered in one of the soldier's ears. That soldier and one other remained to watch over their dead companions until they could be collected.

The remaining soldiers surrounded Sam, Adam, and Jayne, looking very ready to head back to their ship.

Adam was amazed by Jayne. She was hurt but refused all medical services until all the soldiers were treated first. There was no question about how brave she was. If she had missed the banner, it would have all been over. She had so much knowledge about the ways of the galaxy, which fascinated Adam.

Yet there was also a tender side, and of course, she was beautiful. In the old days, it was referred to as being smitten. Adam was in love, the type called love at first sight.

He had never felt this feeling, and it was strong. It surrounded his mind with each thought he had. Jayne was surrounded by the soldiers, with Adam to her right. Sam Smith walked behind them.

Sam Smith's mind was racing with thoughts and scenarios. By the time he arrived at their shuttle, he had made plans for Jayne.

12

LOST AND FOUND

Space is not just huge, it is constantly getting larger. As each second passes by, its entirety is expanding, making each destination point that much further to attain.

Utago was close to the end. He was not conscious yet not dead either.

———

The ship had made a blunder, a rather large mistake that would cost them time. There are, of course, procedures that would prevent it from happening. Accidents usually occur not due to one point of failure. Through a combination of errors and missed actions plus just bad luck, the starship was here. Here being entirely in the wrong area of space.

Its captain was ill and did not oversee the space fold jump. His second in command was performing the jump, which normally would not be an issue.

Typically, two people would be involved via their protocol, thus adding more safety to the action. This time, it was not done as the second in command did not have much respect or faith in the crew and knew that he really did not need a second person.

He made a basic mistake while entering the factors into the ship's computers, which are usually reviewed by another officer before being executed.

While distracted, he acknowledged all the pre-jump messages without reading them. It was during the jump, which was taking much longer than it should have when he realized his mistakes. Once a space fold is initiated, you can't disengage, so he figured he would wait it out and then apply a correction jump.

As soon as the ship finished the jump, a major alarm went off not just in the control room but also in the captain's quarters. It did not take long before the old, sick captain was on the bridge in an especially bad mood.

"What did we hit? There should be no ships in this area!"

The man who was in charge now was all over the monitor screens, finding the answers to the questions just asked.

"We hit an escape tube and are in sector 364. I know it is the wrong area. I made a mistake, sorry."

Now, the old captain was taking it all in, "You made many mistakes. Retrieve the tube and then set the correct course."

"Even if there is someone in that tube, they are long dead now."

The captain was a by-the-book type of person. He also was fast to anger and pushed the communication button to tell the crew to retrieve the tube and use all procedures associated with a tube or pod recovery. Also, to contact him for anything that is pertinent or out of the ordinary.

The captain's anger showed in his eyes like they were dissecting the man in their view. Then his thoughts changed, as did the look in his eyes.

"Create a new jump to get us there as quick as possible. I now have to entertain our guests longer. I will do the confirmation myself."

Their ship was transporting three different races, each staying in their own sections and traveling to their vacation spots. Time always plays a role within the galaxy. He knew two of the three races would not be happy about the delay.

Utago had lost a third of his mass, making him look younger. He was unconscious, resembling a perfectly preserved mummy. His body was now responding to the change in oxygen levels in the air. Acting like a wake-up call, he sat up on the table he was lying on.

This scared the people around him, who had thought he was dead. They fell on each other, trying to get away. Then, one of the medical people placed a translator on his head while the others regained their composure. It was determined that he was just in need of food and drink, which were provided.

The captain was contacted and quickly arrived at the scene. He began with the following.

"Hello, friend. I have some questions for our records, and then we will get you to a transfer station." The captain then asked Utago for his name and how he ended up in an escape tube in the middle of nowhere.

Utago answered, "My name is Utago, and I am on a mission to save Plutoneus."

That caught the captain's attention, as he was an avid follower of the battle between Plutoneus and General Max.

The captain responded, "Were you the one who picked him up after the battle? I heard he died and has not been seen since."

Utago proudly responded, "I was first to him after his fight, and he still lives!"

Now, the captain's attention was fully on Utago as he asked, "Once I empty this ship of passengers, where would you like me to take you? Also, if you would not mind, I would like to hear your complete story.

The captain also wanted pictures of their meeting plus holograms of the event. He then stated the following, "I don't agree with Plutoneus about G-Corp. They are needed, and if not them, there will always be someone else to fill that void. Yet his tenacity and bravery in fighting against them is really something." As he ended, it felt like he was searching for words he could not find.

Utago accepted the captain's offer. He started from the time he had left his home world, meeting Dragonfly and then Plutoneus. His story continued about their quest to find a cure and how they had to abandon ship.

He did not mention the time crystal, nor did he go into details about how he survived in the tube for so long.

Utago, after telling his tale, stated the following.

"I would like to go back to my home world." He then proceeded to explain where it was located in the galaxy.

Little did Utago realize that his dream of becoming "someone" within the galaxy had already begun. The captain was very impressed with Utago's story, which he had now added to with the fact that he had rescued him. Tales were beginning to form about the great Utago.

Utago thought, *it is said that you can never go back home.* This, of course, refers to the philosophical aspects of that statement, not the physical aspects. One can usually retrace the path back to where they started.

All things change, as do people and places. Not only can we not go back home, but even if we could, we would not be the same person who left. It never can feel the same.

When Utago left, most people thought he was crazy. To them, it was like saying you are going to live in the wilderness. For all the lack of freedom in his home world, it was safe. The stories surrounding barbaric incidents around their galaxy kept most very happy to stay there.

Utago had not thought how his return would be received. He imagined it to be a small affair with some friends and family arriving to greet him. His phone still worked, but they were too far away for him to contact anyone.

The captain was feeling better, partly due to the fact he felt he had saved Utago's life. Yet if his second in command had not made the jump mistake, nothing more would have occurred.

So many things are connected to other things, forming a true picture. Our eyes can never see the whole thing, just tiny sections of detail. Never seeing the entirety nor understanding our true place within it.

The captain had contacted Utago's home world with the ship's long-range communications system. Letting them know that Utago was heading home and that their arrival would be in two days.

Time passed quickly, and many wanted Utago's attention. He repeated his story with much more detail than the first telling.

When Utago was in orbit of his home planet, he tried to contact his family and a few friends he had left there, but he received no response. This concerned him as he had not expected much change since his departure from there.

The captain declared he would personally fly the transport, taking Utago home.

Instead of landing at a welcome center, the ship headed towards a field with hundreds of people standing and sitting in front of a makeshift stage. The shuttle landed behind the stage.

When Utago exited the shuttle, there was a stairway at the back leading to the stage floor. He was directed to go up the stairs. There was music playing and a curtain that was hiding the crowd's view of the stage.

Utago was still confused about exactly what was happening. Within minutes of his being backstage, the music stopped, and the announcement was made.

So much had changed within such a short time compared to what he had left behind. Utago now heard his name mentioned, and the crowd roared with approval. He wondered what he had done to receive such a welcome.

His brother was there with others who were strangers to Utago, and they rushed up to him. His brother said, "Utago, it's great seeing you! You have to tell your fans a story. Any story will do. They have paid to see you, please."

Utago answered, mixed with anger, "My fans? They paid to hear me talk. What is going on?"

"I will tell you everything when we go home. Please tell them a story of your adventures." As he said this, he also glanced at the people with him.

Utago was mad, yet there were a lot of people in front of the stage. He would have it out with his brother at home. Now, he had to attend to his "fans".

Once he was at the center of the stage, the front curtains were raised. Utago had to admit it was quite a feeling seeing all those faces coming to see him. Waiting to hear what words he had to say. He decided to tell the tale of when he and Bubba went to the ship in distress to rescue any survivors. How they got attacked by the ship and the rescue that occurred after.

There is nothing like actually being in an event to be able to really describe it. Many descriptions just repeat someone else's description, modifying or adding new elements. Yet these observations can never be like someone who was actually there. Even more so when someone is a direct participant in the action.

Utago had every eye and ear at his command. To his credit, he gave details and insights that only he would know. He was a great orator, a talent he never realized he had. This was also observed by others.

As he ended the story, the crowd demanded more. They started a chant about that desire, which, after some time, became even louder, making it feel like it would have to be responded to affirmatively.

Utago then related how he had met Dragonfly and traveled to Mars, with Plutoneus demanding to see his queen. To Utago, that was what she was, royalty with a twist. There are few in the galaxy that truly appreciate how smart she is.

Finally, he bid goodbye to the crowd, which still demanded more, but this time, it faded quickly. The announcer thanked the crowd for coming, adding that the great Utago would schedule another appearance soon.

It seemed like so many things had changed that Utago felt like a stranger in his own world. That feeling happens to many who travel around the galaxy, and it is a disconnected feeling when returning home.

Utago waited until they had arrived at his brother's home. It was new and quite fancy, being large and having exquisite statues and decorations outside and inside the mansion.

By this time, Utago's thoughts were less filled with emotion and more analytical in nature.

His brother started by saying, "I was contacted about your exploits, so I decided to publish your tales. The books have become best sellers." He finished that statement with a big smile.

Again, Utago's mind was upset with his life being exploited, even if it was his brother, yet he quickly resumed his logical thoughts and asked the following question.

"Who contacted you? How did they contact you?"

"He sent me messages, and I fixed them up to make exciting stories about my brother, the great Utago."

Utago was still just staring at his brother, which made him respond again.

"I don't know who he is. The name he used was EL. He seemed to know all about you and your adventures. He suggested I tell the people about what you have accomplished."

Utago's mind was amazed. He really did not know what he expected to hear, yet with the truth now revealed, harder questions emerged.

Who was this EL? How could he know so much about Utago's story? Especially once he traveled with Jayne and Bubba. He then instructed his brother to retrieve all the private messages sent so he could review the information within them. Also, he wanted all the books his brother had published about him. Before Utago would make more decisions regarding his future plans, he wanted to have a full review of everything now before him.

After a long sleep plus more reading about his exploits, Utago wanted to correct the books that had made him the hero of each event. Surprisingly, the communications from EL were very accurate. It was his brother who had changed the content to his favor.

What was most intriguing was how this EL knew anything, let alone all the facts he had communicated. The messages were untraceable, defeating any physical contact, and as his brother explained, EL always sent messages but never responded to any sent back. There was no question who was in charge, calling the shots.

The next aspect of his returning home that was not expected was his fan club. There were hundreds of people following his adventures, many wanting to live that type of life. It was not like that when he left, just himself and four others, testing themselves and experiencing the galaxy.

Within a few days of his return, the government contacted him to request a meeting. It was insinuated he would be very pleased with what they had to say. It occurred to him that his travels around the galaxy were easier than returning home. There, he was just another traveler, but now he was a celebrity.

There were fans camping out right by the gate of his brother's mansion. Everyone wanted him to do something that really was for them. His brother was setting up another event for him to speak to his admirers. The group outside wanted pictures and autographs, while the government wanted something else.

All societies go through a period of rapid change. Depending on which side of the change you reside, it is a radical departure of normality or something that has finally been accepted, which had taken far too long to occur.

When this happens, the powers in charge have to make hard decisions. There are only three choices to be made, and most resolutions are hybrid combinations of those choices.

The government can try to ignore it, accept it, or eliminate the problem. They sent out a beautiful transport to take Utago to their most valued building. The capital building itself, where all the laws and policies were created.

There were different rooms there, each with a unique name to designate its presence. Then, that room would be decorated following the name given, including the colors and styles of each element within that room.

Utago had never seen the capital until now, never been in any of the famous rooms he had heard about. They entered the Room of Power, given its name by having the most dangerous things their society had and then glorifying them. There were many pictures of their famous leaders in daring events. Pictures of their weapons and models made in their form were used as chairs for the occupants. All items in the room reflected some aspect of power in general. Most were specific to certain people, places, or things.

Sitting in a room like that changed the moment of things. Being in such a special room made all within it feel that power.

There were five people there, not counting Utago, and only one spoke during their meeting.

It started with the leader saying, "Utago, all who enter this room are equals. You have proven yourself to merit being here. We have an offer for you with three stipulations." He paused here to take in Utago body language. There were no clues to be learned, and he continued.

"We will purchase a top-class starship and fully supply it for its first journey. The stipulations are as follows. First, you travel on your own with no connections or allegiance to our planet. Second, you take all who wish to go with you. And third, this applies only to you, that you never return here again!" Now again, he stopped to take full account of what Utago would say.

Utago, to his credit, had what would be called a poker face. There was neither anger nor surprise or any other emotion showing. What-ever he was thinking, only he knew, while everyone else waited to find out.

"I accept." It was a short answer that said all that needed to be conveyed. Utago's mind was in deep thought. It went to the fact that being in space or in a foreign world felt more like home than this place ever would again. Not coming back was not a problem.

Traveling under his own banner was also not an issue. He had never thought of contacting his home world for help. The only slight inconvenience was taking all those who wanted to go. It takes a lot to explore the galaxy and is not for the weak of spirit. Most will regret their decision to come along for either sadness in leaving all they love or just the trials that space life can bring.

Now, the man looked at his four companions in the room with a look that expressed his happiness of multiple problems solved. His thought, *Utago will be gone to never return and hopefully many others who may be problems will go with him.*

"Great, we will handle all the details, including the announcements for any who want to join." Now he had a big smile, feeling he had accomplished everything that was needed and that all would be great in their world.

The meeting ended with them transporting Utago back to his brother's home in an even fancier vehicle than his arrival. He was told it would not take long for all to be ready, so be prepared to leave within a short time.

Utago already missed being in space, outside of his home world's control. He wondered if Jayne and Bubba survived while also missing them and Dragonfly. Everyone was calling him the "Great Utago," which was flattering, yet he continuously reminded himself of who he was.

Utago had the warriors' way. It was a spirit that only a warrior would truly understand.

His thoughts went to Brand Wright, his hero. The longer his travels went on, the more he understood that man. Brand, like himself, was no hero, not a great person, just a traveler trying to do some good. Last, his thoughts went to whether Brand would want to be saved. Having a glorious ending and then not ending, he thought, defeated the whole thing.

After some time that equated to three Earth's weeks, the ship was readily supplied, and many new travelers were boarding. There were not as many as the government had expected, yet there were more than two hundred. Many had given up trying to exist in their home world, with a few true explorers among them.

The starship was a recent model that was more of a battleship than a pleasure vessel, but it had many features that were not typical of a warship. Once in space, the organizing began with who would be working and in what areas and time frames.

Utago had chosen two who he trusted who also had starship training in their background. It was more like a community in space than the way a typical starship was run. They were having a group meeting when Utago was surprised with their proclamation.

His first in charge was reading a list of problems and resolutions when he stated the following.

"It has been proposed and voted unanimously that Captain Utago will now and forever be referred to as King Utago." After this was stated, there was great cheer among all who were there.

Utago had never felt such emotions within himself as he felt now. Just a short time ago, he was closed to death, alone in space, now king to people who have put all their trust in his judgments.

13

SAM, JAYNE, AND LOVE

"I thought he was a good man," Bubba said while looking at Dragonfly.

"He is just like humans," she replied. Bubba just kept looking at her, so she added.

"Most creatures are greedy and selfish, foolish and stupid. You must always assume their worst traits when dealing with them. You are different. You reflect the highest qualities of humanity. If you were not so unique, you would not be here right now."

Bubba, for the first time, realized how deeply Dragonfly hated other beings.

She continued, "We will make our move on the next planet's cycle. I have been making arrangements for our rescue mission. Where she is being held has a very high level of security, so there are many elements to arrange."

Bubba lamented, "The waiting is killing me, Jayne is truly special. She always treated me like a captain."

Then Dragonfly gave a serious look and tone, saying, "Bubba Jones, you *are* a Captain!" From that moment on, she always addressed him as Captain Jones.

Dragonfly then showed surprise, an emotion rarely shown by her, and said, "Captain Jones, look at this!" With that, she hit a switch, and the entire wall turned into a video screen.

"This has happened less than 10 minutes ago. Now we have a bigger problem. She is with Sam Smith."

Bubba watched all the action, amazed at Jayne's bravery and agility in her escape.

Dragonfly questioned, "How did he know?"

Bubba quickly understood her dilemma and responded, "Maybe he was just lucky."

Dragonfly gave him a look while thinking, *how did he ever beat me?* "Sam Smith just happened to be on the right planet, at the right location and time, just when all the action was happening, and then able to help assist in finishing Jayne's escape attempt. No, there is something else happening here."

She focused on Adam, and her brain realized the connection. She decided to explain it to Bubba partly to prove him wrong and also to show her brilliance.

"That is an RB, Subject 107, Adam Knight. He has clairvoyance but had never been used in the field." Her thoughts went to Sam Smith, being impressed by his use of resources. He like Brand Wright, always appeared when least expected while also foiling her plans. As much as she wanted to deny it, there was a growing respect for her hated nemesis.

Bubba knew that Dragonfly was incredibly smart, and it was hard to really relate to people who have photographic memories. Yet still, the speed of her analysis of the current situation was truly impressive.

"We will have to shadow them until the time is right to make our move. He is on a star-battleship, so it will take just a little longer before Jayne is back with us."

Bubba was again amazed at how little this major event affected her. It was like someone else having a street closed and just a bit annoyed driving through the detour. He was aware of her deep hatred for Sam

Smith, which worried him that her intentions to save Jayne and desire to kill Sam may cause an unsuccessful outcome to their rescue attempt.

———

When the power of love really takes over, it becomes all-encompassing. Each thought acknowledges and conforms to its force. How will it affect my most precious? Images of new experiences, even if experienced before, become surrounded and enhanced by the mutual connection to that event.

It has been said that the greatest adventures are shared. How much greater are they then with the person you love the most?

Adam and Jayne, plus all the others, alive and dead, were now back on the star-battleship. Sam Smith had immediately left the others going into his room, which was quite luxurious, being uninterested in Jayne.

He had already concluded that she had the Jinn. Maybe he was contemplating how to take it from her, which would not be hard. Whatever his thoughts were for the next three weeks, they just stayed in orbit on full alert, with Sam Smith not speaking to anyone.

Adam had never really felt that type of love. It was pleasurable yet painful. All he wanted to do was be around Jayne. She was so many things, a puzzle within an enigma.

That is the nature of women to men. A mystery that is so beautiful, even when following it to a knowable doom, it is done smiling. Adam knew that her feelings were not as strong as his own. With his abilities, he could feel the future would bring sadness and sorrow, yet being near the love of his life was all that mattered.

Jayne had special feelings for Adam. He was right there when she needed him the most. Love for Jayne was serving a purpose, a greater need than one's own pleasure. She liked being around Adam, but her mission was always first in her mind.

She was expecting an interview or some type of inquisition. To her surprise, that didn't happen. Adam stayed near her and asked her many questions, just not the kind that would review important mission information. That would throw her off, the questions were as follows:

What was her favorite color, what type of food did she like, and many other things in that order?

The temptation to use the Jinn kept getting stronger as her will-power weakened. In her mind, she went from prisoner to prisoner with just much friendlier jailers. She was free to do whatever she wanted on the ship. Everyone there, including the captain, was waiting for Sam Smith to give the orders.

That was the talk, where would they go next and when would that happen. Finally, Sam wanted to talk with Jayne. It appeared to all aboard that this would get them moving on to wherever they were bound.

When Jayne entered the private library, Sam was sitting on a chair, and another identical one was waiting for her to use. She figured he did not want to share any secrets she may reveal.

"My name is Sam Smith, and I work with the US government. I don't expect you to believe anything I say, but I am here to help you. Where would you like me to take you?"

"Thank you for the offer, but all I need is a starship, and I will get on my way," Jayne said very politely with a smile to end her statement.

Now very out of character for Sam Smith, his persona was changing, he responded.

"Dear Jayne, I fear too many are after you. Without a battleship, your chances of survival are very low. I will not have that on my conscience. Please let me help."

Jayne, taken by his seeming concern, answered, "Besides Gentry Lord, there are no others after me, and I don't fear him."

Sam's facial expression said nothing. His voice was soft but firm, "We both know you have a great prize that many might be after you for it. I myself wanted it at one time, but not anymore."

Jayne was now white. Her secret was known by this man. He was the most powerful person on the ship, and he knew about the Jinn. She realized that she would have to play along, at least for now. What else could she do?

Then Sam, seeing fear appear on her face, said, "Only I know about it on this ship. I surmise Gentry Lord was getting close to finding out. Yet there are others who also know that some secrets can only be contained so tightly. Where do you want to go?"

Jayne looked at Sam Smith, thinking this man, who knows so much and has ultimate power, asking her for orders. He reminded her of the short time she had spent with Brand. Like Sam Smith, he knew so much about so many things, yet he cared about her.

"Did you know CW?" Asked Jayne.

Sam Smith let a smile slip out. "I called him Subject 9," then he chuckled and continued.

"He makes an impression. I am on your side. I know you want to get to the Nevermore."

Jayne had so many emotions that each shined in its own light. With her eyes fixed on Sam Smith, she whispered, "Thank you."

Sam Smith was changing. The feeling of doing good things for certain people, with no desire for personal reward, it was a new sensation.

Once she left, Adam was waiting to be with her. He could not help himself. Any moments spent with his obsession were a great minute spent.

Jayne gave him a hug and kiss on the cheek, her demeanor being totally different than before the meeting.

"I guess the sit down went good," Adam said with a huge smile, partly still reliving the hug and kiss.

"It did. He reminds me of CW a bit. Are you hungry?"

Adam was happy for her happiness yet jealous of all the men she was fond of. This was so unlike his general happy-go-lucky manner. Strong love will change people, hopefully for the better, yet the other side will also happen.

He started to think she had a thing for older men, and this upset him. His rational mind stated it was an absurd conclusion, and his RB abilities also did not register any truth to that thought. What was true was that these feelings and thoughts were not the Adam Knight he identified with.

As they were eating lunch, Adam realized he knew virtually nothing about the history of the Nevermore, where Jayne had grown up. She was happy to tell the story, which he listened to without interruptions. Just hearing her voice, seeing her looking into his eyes, he could listen for an eternity, was how he was feeling.

Jayne explained it from her perspective, so it was very skewed to her politics.

"It really reminds me of an Earth story, the one called Robin Hood." Then she giggled. Adam had never seen her so relaxed.

She continued, "Let me start with the players, and I will fill in the needed details. This galaxy is served by many suppliers, but one is the largest and controls many planets and resources. They are the Galaxy Corporation, which we call the G-Corp. They also have their own army called Galaxy Force."

At this point, Adam said, "Which you call G-Force!" Smiling at his beloved.

Now Jayne chastised him with a turned-up face, saying, "No, we called them GFs. Now, I will continue. Our captain, CW, decided to help a planet that needed medicine but did not have the funds to purchase it. The planet that did have it was close, so we picked it up and delivered it to those who needed it. From then on, we were an outlaw ship to the Space Force from Earth and to G-Corp. CW was always a step ahead of them both. At times, the luckiest events happened, bringing victory from defeat. In some worlds, we were treated like royalty, yet most would not even acknowledge our presence. The Nevermore has saved planets and helped so many worlds, then CW was betrayed and lost to us all."

At that point, she stopped to hear Adam's response.

Before Adam could say a word, the ship's battle alarm system started screaming.

14

UNDER ATTACK

People instantly were running in all directions. Moving quickly but not banging into each other, they had their areas that needed their attention.

For a moment, Adam was frozen in thought and action, then Jayne, grabbing his arm, said as she moved quickly, "We're going to the bridge."

Even though Adam had spent more time on that ship, Jayne knew where the important areas were, and she moved quite quickly. She had let go of his arm and he was now following in her wake.

Once they had received permission to enter the command center, Sam Smith was there. The situation was grim. There were three Galaxy Corp warships in front of them. Also, there was a much smaller attack ship behind them with Gentry Lord's forces ready to attack.

They were surrounded and outnumbered when they received the message from one of the ships in front of them.

"Transfer Jayne Stillwater now, or we will destroy your ship and all aboard. I will give you 10 seconds to reply."

All eyes were on Sam Smith, who was now standing in the center of the command center. Looking at the captain, he said the following.

"Fire on the center ship." It was said calmly. The weapons officer looked at the captain for acknowledgment, for some sign of agreement.

The captain said and did nothing. It appeared he wanted to try and talk his way out of the situation at hand.

Now Sam Smith was mad, yelling, "Fire on them now!" Nothing was happening with the seconds ticking away. It seemed all the soldiers were frozen, waiting for their captain to confirm the order.

The next few seconds seemed like eons, waiting when there was no time to wait. Just as the captain said fire, their destruction began.

There were two distant explosions within the ship, with a third coming from the rear of the vessel. Four shots were fired on Sam Smith's battleship. Being in the command center, it had better reinforcements but would not hold up long.

Now, the captain, treating time like a precious commodity, said quickly, suggesting Sam Smith, Adam, and Jayne get on an escape ship that was attached below the command center. There was complete mayhem on the ship, with most things not working, but what was showing was only bad indicators.

Sam Smith was a strange man, being unpredictable among many other traits. One thing he was making perfectly clear, he was not afraid to die. He turned to Jayne and Adam and said the following.

"You are both free to make your own choices. I am staying on this ship." He said it calmly, which was incredible, considering all the chaos around him.

Adam wanted to take the escape ship, yet he said nothing, waiting for Jayne to respond. Jayne also seemed rather calm, given the gravity of their situation. Adam started to realize these people had been close to death before. He imagined that being close and surviving it would make you braver the next time around.

"I will stay with you." Jayne stared directly at Sam Smith. She was thinking about using the Jinn. She wanted to do it, but something inside her kept saying not now.

The sound of those words made Adam angry. Why would she risk her life here on this ship moments from destruction? Why did she not ask what he thought was best to do? Did she not care about him? These foolish thoughts were in his head.

Then Jayne turned to Adam, with her eyes locked into his, "My dear Adam, this is my life. If not here, it would have happened on the Nevermore. Please, Adam, take the escape ship. Your life is my reward."

With those words Adam felt terrible with all his crazy thoughts. It is so hard to know what someone really feels or thinks. His clairvoyance abilities told him the ship does not have long before it become space junk. And yet he did not move. He was more than willing to die right there with his newly beloved. He brought her into an embrace, feeling her heartbeat.

"I will be by your side." There was a smile on his face and peace in his heart. Such is the power of love that when the world is on fire, all that matters is your true love by your side.

————

Dragonfly was intense, especially when she was building something that Bubba believed was a weapon. There was a factory on her ship, and she had been designing parts on her computer, and then they were created below.

The computer she was using was much more advanced than Earth's models. It had a holographic projection that could be manipulated by the user's hands. Once that stage was done, the fabrication process began.

It was physically produced and assembled, which then needed to be attached to the front of the ship. It involved some outside work in space plus inside modifications on the ship.

Bubba had been forgotten during this time and had free roam of the ship and all that resided within. A few times, he asked her when and how they were going to get Jayne from Sam Smith's battleship. She only said she was working on a plan that involved what she was currently doing.

Bubba was able to get a fix on Sam Smith's ship, which was just in orbit around LaTaFree. He wondered why Sam had not left while assuming he was waiting for something.

It was nearly three weeks when Dragonfly finally stated that she was ready to get Jayne back.

She instructed Bubba to get into a space suit, which instantly made him ask, "Are we going into space and breaking into their ship?"

His innocence always delighted Dragonfly, and with a sweet smile, she replied.

"No, Captain Jones. We are going into silent mode. Everything, including life support, will be turned off. There are many ways to detect a ship in space unless that ship generates no electrical frequencies. Then, it is by sight alone. They will never see us coming."

Dragonfly personally strapped him into a seat in the command center, stating that when the action happens, they will need to be very secure.

Bubba had no idea what was coming, yet in his defense, she was going to show the galaxy a weapon never seen before. Then he asked an obvious question.

"If everything is turned off and their ship is still moving, how will we figure out where they are located?"

Dragonfly loved it when people appreciated her brilliance.

"I am going to approximate where they will be, and then, like an arrow shot in the night, we become invisible until we reach the target."

Bubba just gave her a look of astonishment. She was so positive about her abilities. It was more than that. She truly believed in herself and treated most things like a game. She could easily be childish, making one forget how smart she really was. And then there was the killer side of her personality. He had never actually seen it, but between the stories he was told and her hatred for most beings, it was always there in his mind.

Once she set the last controls, everything changed. It felt as if the ship had died. The darkness was a blackness that hid everything within it. Seeing no lights flashing or blinking just felt so strange. Also, there were no sounds. Ships of that size always had a hum about them. They are never completely silent.

As they sped through the black sky in silence, it was equally black and silent inside. Bubba could feel the energy in not just the air but in time. Each second, they moved in the dark the intensity grew in anticipation of their outcome.

Soldiers know this feeling of being on the edge of life and death well. You will never be as alive as when death is within a moment's minute. It brings sense to their peak performance.

Bubba now realized he did not know if there was anything he needed to do. Knowing Dragonfly, she liked to rely on her own calculations and abilities, making him just a spectator to her brilliance.

The flip side of them not being able to see Dragonfly's ship coming towards them was also true for Dragonfly and Bubba seeing Sam Smith's battleship. They were both gazing out the main window, looking into the dark for a sign of something.

One of the abilities of Dragonfly's mind was being able to grasp all the elements of a situation very quickly and deal with a resolution far faster than almost everyone. If you ever had to debate her, it would be a very humiliating experience.

Dragonfly's surprise scream, which she would never admit to, brought Bubba out from inside his thoughts to the current scene unfolding. At first, he could hardly see anything, thinking her eyesight must be superior to a human. Then it started to become clear, too clear, as they were rapidly approaching three G-Corp battleships plus Sam Smith's battleship, plus another much smaller craft behind Sam Smith's vessel.

Then, just as Dragonfly was starting the new weapon, a fifth ship arrived. It also was behind Sam Smith's vessel, facing the smaller ship there.

That is when Bubba saw Sam Smith's battleship badly damaged, to the point that parts were breaking off as it was cracking apart. His heart now went to Jayne, praying she was still all right. He felt the guilt of each action he commanded that brought pain and trouble to her.

What happened next froze all the ships except Dragonfly's vessel for a complete minute. That minute was more than enough to change everything.

————

It is said ultimate power corrupts those who acquire it. Yet it does not have to be ultimate. Combined with obsession leads to poor judgment, which can be seen by all except the person wielding it.

Gentry Lord was not thinking properly when he called Galactic Corporation and made a deal to regain possession of Jayne Stillwater. If that was not bad enough, then physically going on a ship to be there when the transfer happened was just too dangerous.

His advisors tried to talk him out of going, but he laughed at them, stating there would be three Galactic Battleships there, and soon he would get new advisors.

————

King Utago was headed to LaTaFree. He had received a message that a big event would happen there. He planned one large space fold jump and then full speed to the target.

————

Dragonfly had activated all the power on her ship and was now working the controls of both the new weapon and her ship's course. She was heading up from below towards the center ship of the Galactic fleet.

The weapon first looked like a snake's tongue but had four to five tips at its end. It was a huge laser beam that also had the characteristics of a whip in the way it moved about. It was 30 feet wide, and the length varied as it moved around in space, from 100 to 150 feet.

The most amazing aspect was how much energy it was using. The beam licked the bottom of the middle ship, and it split it apart like a hot knife through butter. The ship's shields were no defense to its onslaught.

At that point, everyone watching was expecting the beam to cease, either needing to be recharged or at least lesson the energy after the first G-Corp battleship was destroyed. Not only did it not shut down, but it also seemed to become even larger in width and length.

Then Dragonfly spun her ship around and sliced the next ship in half. It happened very quickly, and that was when all the other ships started to respond.

The remaining G-Corp battleship was now using full power to escape. They were trying to do a space jump. The ship's movement was slower than the speed of the light chasing them. It had overtaken the craft and then, looking almost like a hand, crushed the back of the ship, rendering it inoperable.

At that point, Gentry Lord started to grasp fully what was happening and who was next. His vessel did not have space-fold technology, so it went to its fastest speed, heading away from the destruction it had just witnessed.

He was alerted that the other ship was also following them away from the action. At first, it did not directly connect to Gentry that it was their enemy. Once it fired upon them, destroying their limited shields plus disabling the engines, Gentry opened a channel to communicate with them.

"This is Gentry Lord, supreme commander of planetary security for LaTaFree. Immediately end your attack before this becomes a galactic incident. If you harm me, there will be repercussions."

Utago himself had operated the navigator's chair and also fired on Gentry Lord. His crew watched, none of them ever fired on another vessel. They were in awe of their King. Scared, proud, and had so many feelings, with the most being that *I could never have done that.*

"I am King Utago and care not about who you are or where you are from. You attacked a friend of mine, which was a fatal mistake on your part. Say your goodbyes to whatever divinities you talk to."

"Stop, please. Let me make amends. Surely, there is a deal to be made between us. King Utago, it was not my weapons that brought its destruction."

Utago was not just strong and quick of movement. He was smart and replied with the following.

"No, you contacted the ships that attacked my friends. You're wasting your last moments. Accept your fate with dignity. We all shall pass to the other side." With that, he closed the line of communication.

Not a word was spoken in King Utago's command center. He had killed many compared to most, it is the warrior's way. As he waited, knowing Gentry was calling for help, he thought about how everything is controlled by time.

He looked at his crew. They were book readers and daytime adventurers, now seeing what it was really like. No one said a word of objection to what was coming next. They were totally committed to their King.

As more time went by, Utago's thoughts went to the fact that no reinforcements were coming for Gentry. He must have made many enemies. Utago would be his last in that line.

He pushed some buttons, and Gentry Lord was gone, buried in the vastness of space.

"Take us back to the target ship," Utago commanded.

15

CELEBRATION

Before, it would have been futile to use the escape ships or pods with three battleships looming about. Now, with all three disabled and working on their own problems, the escape from Sam Smith's ship was underway.

Dragonfly had turned off her new weapon, and Utago's ship was also there, providing hailing to all for their rescue.

Jayne and, of course, Adam, who never left her side, were with Sam and two other soldiers who were protecting Sam, plus a pilot and communications expert.

First, Jayne heard Utago's message, and her heart pounded for joy.

Her face was glowing as she said, "Thank all that is good, my Utago, King Utago is alive and well. We must go to his ship." Before anyone could say a word, another message came through from a different ship.

"This is Captain Jones. We are ready and able to take anyone that needs rescuing."

Jayne again looked like she was in her happiest state as she proclaimed, "Captain Jones is also alive. How wonderful! I must talk to him!" She felt bad about her threat to kill him, being her last words before parting.

Then, they all looked at Jayne, who instructed them to go to Utago's ship.

King Utago initiated private communication with Dragonfly. Dragonfly answered his holographic call with matching technology. It appeared that they were in one room together. Their complete bodies were there. Every facial movement could be seen in incredible detail.

"King Utago, you have done very well on your own, making short work to become a king."

"Dragonfly, thank you. I would like you to join us in our celebration. I have only one request, that you kill no one while on my ship."

Utago could see she was hurt by his words. He continued, "Agreed?"

"Is that how you see me, just a killer that needs constraints?"

Utago replied, "I see you as a Queen, the most intelligent person in the galaxy who needs no one. Powerful and cunning, at levels that all cannot even imagine."

Now, she responded, "I agree. What time is the party," showing a bright face with little giggles.

There was a round table with each person's name in front of their plates. It was a fancy room yet had odd dimensions. King Utago had Sam Smith to his right and Dragonfly to his left. Next to Sam Smith was Adam Knight, who, along with Jayne Stillwater and Bubba Jones, completed the circle back to Dragonfly.

Utago stood up, and the horizontal wall to his left converged with the other vertical walls, revealing a huge banquet hall. Utago's table was on a platform overlooking more than 30 similar tables that spread out below his.

The others who were there consisted of people on Sam Smith's battleship plus personnel from King Utago's ship. Many of those were people who had some function in the events that just happened. Others were people who were on Utago's ship but mostly as passengers.

They were being served by members of Utago's subjects, who looked upon it as an honor to be able to serve the people who were risking their lives for a noble cause.

He rose, looking at the tables that stretched out before him, and then said the following.

"Friends, we are here today to celebrate our victory and the people who made it happen. Beginning with Sam Smith and Adam Knight." Then he turned to his right, extending his right arm and pointing to Sam and Adam.

"They were in the exact right place and time to help our heroine Jayne escape her prison on LaTaFree. No matter what situation she is in, her bravery and courage plus focus and willpower always prevail." Then he pointed to Jayne, who appeared to be embarrassed by all of Utago's words.

"Of course, there is also our hero, Captain Jones, who never stops surprising and impressing while also defeating each enemy he has encountered."

The crowd below yelled words of approval as each person was mentioned.

Then Utago looked directly at Dragonfly and said, "None of this would be possible without this person, without her brilliance of mind and courage beyond measure. She is the reason we are all here together alive, the deciding factor in our victory today. I present you, Dragonfly."

The crowd that was sitting below now on their feet, shouted their level of approval, which was deafening. It was twice as loud as all before and lasted three times as long.

Dragonfly looked at the crowd, for she and Bubba were the closest to the edge of the stage and the audience below. She had never experienced what was now taking place. She was never admired except by a few, whom she paid as servants or bought something. This was different. Seeing all those people sending love her way changed her in that instant.

For the first time, she was feeling love for other beings. Just the feeling of love was so strange and then for so many. Just minutes ago, it would have seemed incredulous for that to happen.

Then Utago quieted the crowd to give his final remark before the feast began.

"Let us have a moment of silence for our friends and foes who no longer are here with us. There is a great battle between light and darkness. We fight for the light. It must be defended. We take no joy in our enemies' demise. We did what had to be done."

Then, after a long minute, he finished with, "Now let us celebrate!"

The next few hours were wonderful for all that were there. It was the reward for all their sacrifices. The fact that these types of times come rarely is what makes them so special. The stories of where you were and what you were doing, meeting people you have saved and those that have saved you.

Knowing that you and everyone around you have made it to another day. People in war know that feeling too well.

Special times like that are never lost. They become the markers of our lives.

It was agreed that the next day, they would set up a strategy on how best to complete their mission.

The reality was that Jayne was making Adam's choice. He would only go wherever she went. Sam Smith had contacted Earth, who was sending a ship for his return.

Both Dragonfly and Utago's ships would head together to reach the Nevermore.

Captain Jones would stay with Dragonfly as Jayne decided to go with King Utago. Initially, when Bubba heard her decision, he was disappointed, yet he could understand why she would choose Utago over him.

He was the master of his ship, and he also had a proven record of being able to handle trouble when it arrived. Still, he now longed for the "Good old days" while he was captain of them both.

Jayne had apologized profusely over her statement to kill him on sight. While he looked at her, there was an unspoken communication about their mutual secret. A passing of the touch, like in a relay race, the baton had been exchanged.

There was an argument between Sam Smith and Adam.

"Adam, if I leave you here, you may never get back to Earth!"

"I don't care," replied Adam, said very adamantly.

Sam Smith then changed his approach to try to demand his acceptance.

"Sir, you are my responsibility. You are a guest of the United States government, and with that, there are certain restrictions that apply."

"Unless you are planning to physically restrain me-"

Sam, now losing patience, interrupted with, "That is an option!"

Adam continued, "Then you might as well kill me, for I will never help you and try to expose all I have seen. I am staying with Jayne!"

Sam knew he was right. Adam was in love, and that power trumped all other thoughts and actions. He wished him well and hoped to see him back on Earth at some future time.

Sam Smith's rescue ship arrived, and the survivors of the last vessel piled into the current ship with two less-than-expected. Sam Smith and Adam both staying with Jayne.

They became a fleet with Utago's ship leading and Dragonfly following. It was assumed by most Jayne would be better at locating her former ship, the Nevermore.

Bubba, however, figured Dragonfly would find the Nevermore first. Her genius was better appreciated when being around her. He now understood clearly why Utago was so impressed with her.

His thoughts went to Brand Wright, his friend, and how different he had become because of it. Never in his wildest fantasies did he imagine all he had seen and experienced happened just by knowing one man.

He wondered what Brand would be like if they were able to fix him and bring him back to his old self, if he would even be thankful for all that was needed to make it happen.

Then another thought entered his brain, that something much bigger was coming, and they were all small pawns in bringing it to reality. Even Brand was just a player on that board, getting into the right position to attack. Bubba chuckled to himself regarding how crazy it sounded even to himself.

16

NEVERMORE

The Core was the real power within the Galactic Corporation empire. Their number of members changed, and sometimes, there were a few more or fewer participants at the table. Currently, there were seven entities, some of which were from different races of beings. Four were from the home planet where the Galactic Corporation started. The three others, from different races of beings, were invited to the group for their individual achievements.

There were many positive revelations, yet with all the good news, there are always problems. On the plus side, they had retrieved Plutoneus's time capsule, which would work into their final execution of that problem. Also, in that regard, it had disrupted most of the rebels associated with the Nevermore. Soon, that entire problem would be gone.

Their businesses were doing very well, and they were acquiring more planet governments.

What seemed like a simple extraction, given they had amassed overpowering forces against the vessel containing the person, Jayne Stillwater, had failed. Most things are never as simple as they may appear, with hidden connections that ripple as when a rock is thrown into a lake.

Not only did the extraction fail, but they also lost all three battle-ships sent. The weapon that destroyed them did it within a minute and had never been witnessed before. Instead of sending immediate backup, it was decided this needed to be examined further before any response would be initiated.

———

The new fleet consisting of Utago and Dragonfly ships had taken three space fold jumps, putting them close to the edge of the galaxy. Dragonfly was the first to detect the Nevermore doing it by a totally different method than Jayne.

She left the communications to Jayne regarding setting up their meeting to finally give Brand Wright his cure.

Bubba was just shaking his head from side to side with a big smile. He said, "Never really thought this would happen. Feels almost not real."

Dragonfly, whose feelings for Bubba just kept growing, replied.

"Captain Jones, if not for you, it would never be happening. These things are never over until they are."

She looked at him with a let's wait and see attitude. He wondered if she knew more than she was saying.

Jayne contacted the Nevermore, expecting a larger greeting than she received. It was agreed that all would board, including Dragonfly, Bubba, and four guards to protect their King. Utago wanted to go on his own, yet his people almost demanded that he have protection just in case the unknown happened.

The strange thing was it just felt like everything was wrong. The Nevermore's crew should have been happier, or maybe just more ex-cited to see their return.

There was something that was hard to define, and yet the senses knew it was there. It did not matter. After all they had just experienced, there was no hesitation in seeing its finale.

At first, everything appeared normal. They were warmly greeted after arriving on the Nevermore. Jayne, Adam, Sam Smith, and King Utago plus four guards, arrived first with Dragonfly and Captain Jones shortly thereafter. Once they had all arrived, they were taken to one of the briefing rooms located within the ship.

That was when the first signs of abnormality happened. There were soldiers lined up behind the one long table in the room. On each side of the table, with their backs to the walls, the soldier's weapons were ready and waiting. The current speaker was no one Jayne was aware of, as the captain and others were not present.

She began with, "Congratulations on your successful mission. Once you provide us the Jinn, we will finish what needs to be done." She did not really say it directly to anyone, just to everyone, without making eye contact with her audience.

Bubba, who was keeping an eye on Jayne, instantly replied, acting like he had the Jinn.

"Now, hold on right there. I will use the Jinn once I am next to Brand's time lock." And then adding, "No negotiations on that!"

Now, the speaker's attention was full on Bubba. Her eyes had narrowed, and you could tell she was calculating her next moves.

"Mr. Jones..."

Before she could finish, both Jayne and Dragonfly almost at the exact same time, interrupted shouting, "Captain Jones!"

It was said with such passion that it threw her off, and she began again.

"*Captain* Jones, that will be impossible since his time capsule is no longer on this ship." With that, what was a bad situation became a whole lot worse. Now, eyes were staring at each group, and the air had an electrical feeling as the tension had risen. Only the sounds of heavy breathing were being heard by different people within the room.

The soldiers were ready to kill the people sitting at that table. King Utago's guard also now had their hands on their weapons with their fingers ready to pull the triggers.

You can tell when someone is ready to kill. It is a look in the eyes. First, it appears like a blank, far-off stare. But if you keep looking, it becomes a cold *I care nothing about you* feeling. You can feel the vibrations of death staring back at you.

For some, their breathing became heavy and hard, while others looked and sounded like they were not breathing at all. The real tell was in the hands, always being close to their weapons if not already within their grasp, fingers wrapped around triggers, itching to squeeze the first shot.

In ways, like someone's favorite addiction, just sitting in front of them waiting for their response.

Bubba, who had risen from his seat, his big frame an easy target for any in the room, to his credit, did not scare easily. It just made him more defiant.

The speaker, who never introduced herself, now was looking only at Bubba as she smiled with evil and spoke.

"None of you will get out of this room alive unless I have the Jinn. There is no escaping your situation. I was going to kill your companions first until you gave it up. Now, though, I have changed my mind."

Then, with a sneer, said, "Captain Jones, are you ready to die?"

Within a second of that, all the lights went off, and really everything became dead regarding the ship's functions. After a complete two seconds, the backup system finally tried to illuminate the situation. Just as the primary systems had failed now, the backups were struggling to stay lit as they flickered to dark.

And in that moment, the action started. Utago had his gun in hand, firing the first shots, with Dragonfly following. The fact that King Utago's guards were there provided immeasurable help in keeping their King alive.

Then, so many flashes went off, and with the lights flickering, most fired at Bubba or the chair or wall in front of each participant.

Bubba was an easy target, being big and standing when the lights went off. Jayne instinctively moved as soon as the blackness started. She also pulled Adam with her as she moved under the table. It was one of the safest places at that moment to be.

Sam Smith had already taken a fatal shot, for he did not move fast enough when it became dark within the room.

Between Utago, his guards, and Dragonfly, they were a deadly team against their enemies. Dragonfly had an energy weapon that was so strong it made a hole through seven soldiers it encountered.

It had the power to move from target to target, changing course slightly to make a fatal kill shot on each victim. The soldiers were standing in a straight line, yet her weapon was so intense and deadly that it was very impressive.

Utago had killed three soldiers before he received a bad wound, yet still was fighting regardless of the pain and injury. His guards were brave but inexperienced in close quarters fighting and were more body shields for their King than effective killers.

Bubba had a body force field that was taking multiple hits yet withstanding the onslaught. Dragonfly also had the same defense, which had unlimited power to protect the wearer.

Then, a loudspeaker started demanding total surrender, that there was no way out of the conference room. By this time, it was totally dark, with only people having night vision being able to fire with any type of accuracy.

Dragonfly had reached Bubba, pulling him towards her and into one of the corners of the room.

Now, Jayne and Adam, because of the complete darkness, were blind to all that was happening around them. They were hugging each other while trying to lay as close to the floor as possible.

Adam was then hit by a soldier who had been shot and was lying on the ground. He was firing blindly, and one energy blast hit both Adam and Jayne. Adam had taken the majority of its power, yet Jayne was still feeling sick from its effects.

For a moment before Adam was hit, she had thought about using the Jinn, but she didn't know what to ask for and how to phrase it correctly. Then, with all the action, the thought had faded.

Now her Adam was dead. Sam Smith also had the same fate. Utago was badly injured, and his death was not far off. Jayne, for the first time, realized how much she truly cared for Adam. Not until his demise did the extent of her feelings touch her heart.

Saving CW was important, yet this man loved her. He had risked his life to save and be near her. Then, she thought to herself, *how have I repaid him for all he has done and the risks he has taken for my sake?* Anger enraged her thoughts, I will not let Adam die. I will save them all. I have the Jinn and can fix this.

Dragonfly had modified her time crystals to create two energy shields for Bubba and herself. The strength of the unlimited energy that they were producing could counteract anything entering their fields. She also had a gun for herself based on the time crystal technology, which had never-ending extreme power.

She had worked Bubba and herself into a corner, which provided more coverage than being in any open area of the room. When the speaker started to attack Bubba, she activated her computer virus, which brought the ship down. She was planning on walking out of the room with Bubba and shooting their way back to their ship. Of course, she would activate an attack from her vessel to help with their escape.

Dragonfly was aware that Sam Smith had died. She also knew that Utago would perish shortly as he did not look good. She was using a form of eye enhancement that allowed her to see in the darkness. Jayne and Adam, she was unsure about, yet realized they would not have much time left and even less once leaving this room.

She decided that only Bubba and herself had a chance to make it out alive.

Jayne now was crying over the loss of her Adam. Apologizing to the dead about how really important he was to her life and how things will be different once they are back together again.

Most in that room were now dead. Even Jayne was quickly moving in that direction from multiple blasts around her, each partial effect taking a bit more of the body's life force.

With her own life only minutes away, she pulled out the watch from under her shirt.

Again, the blue mist came out from the antique watch. Time seemed to stop, and her pain was now gone. The young man looked down at his mistress, and it appeared he was troubled by her distress.

"My dear mistress, surely now you are ready for your wish. What does your heart desire?"

Jayne's head, now feeling quite clear and lucid, had finally received the thoughts she had been waiting for. The answer to all her problems became easy, and she said the following.

"This is my wish, that Sam Smith, Adam Knight, Captain Jones, King Utago and his guards, Dragonfly, and myself move back in time a day before we arrive at the Nevermore, and even though we have traveled back 24 hours from this event, we will all retain the memories that we now have."

Then Jayne added as an afterthought.

"You are aware of all the people I have mentioned?"

"Yes, dear mistress. Your request is not hard to do. You realize that you will not get another wish once you move backward in time."

Now Jayne, feeling relieved, responded, "That is not a problem."

The Jinn moved his hands in a dramatic gesture, and in the next moment, Jayne was back on Utago's ship. Her beloved Adam, she now was the one who would not leave his side, was alive again.

They quickly began to talk about their memories with each other. The fact they all had similar experiences solidified their thoughts after contacting Dragonfly and Bubba. New plans needed to be created.

17

TRUTHS REVEALED

They all meet in a virtual meeting room. It was very similar to what Utago had used when talking with Dragonfly. This time, it had brighter lights and a table where they were all seated.

To Bubba, it felt like everyone was really there together. The details in everything from their hair to skin tones truly amazed him. Even everyone's speech sounded exactly as if they were there in person.

Utago spoke first, and his words were hard but true. He was now using a translator, which had thrown Bubba off. Utago was quite eloquent in his words and timing of speech.

"Friends, I must speak words that will be hard to hear, yet also must be spoken. Plutoneus, I fear, is lost to us now. Endangering more lives in an attempt to bring back our friend would be wrong."

With that, there was a deep silence before Sam Smith spoke.

"I agree." That was all he said, keeping with his short nature of dialogue.

Now Jayne spoke up in disagreement. "Just because we had setbacks doesn't mean we should quit. He is that important!" She looked around for support, only to find Adam looking at her eyes. He was her man, willing to go to whatever ends to please her. It was plain to all that his heart was not in that venture, yet he gave a nod of approval to his beloved.

Most were now looking at Bubba. What thoughts did he have? Especially Dragonfly, who had the most intense look there, staring at her Captain Jones.

Bubba, realizing that it was his time to speak and feeling his words would make a difference, looked sad with his head slightly down, and finally spoke.

"He is my best friend, and I have been carrying a secret that now needs to be told. I know what Brand would want us to do, which I have chosen not to do. Now, it needs to be done. I am ashamed for not telling sooner."

The quietness in the room was not heard but felt. Like everyone's breathing had stopped, and all eyes were on one fixed target.

"He wrote a letter, his last wishes if he did not make it back. I have that letter, and he clearly states he does not want anyone risking their lives to save his."

With that, Bubba looked like he had a weight taken from his chest. That secret had aged him in ways that life on Earth never had.

Dragonfly's eye had a tear. She wiped it off fast, in a way that seemed very nonchalant.

Utago, looking at Bubba with deep disappointment, "Plutoneus, last wishes you kept secret?" He asked in a way that made the answer, whatever that answer would be, bad.

Dragonfly quickly interjected herself, saying, "King Utago, if anyone here knows that a person makes their own choices, which is the right of existence. You have made yours for your reasons, as has Captain Jones. You have no right to judge another's choice. Just the right to stay or leave, not to know what lies in someone's heart."

At that moment, Dragonfly showed more humanity than she had ever been given. Her spiritual growth soared to new heights as her mind rearranged many things. Now, she looked at Jayne.

"Dear Jayne, you are not wrong. Brand Wright is that important, yet we have witnessed the death of many here at this table. Consider this second chance for exactly what it is, truly appreciating the present.

The loss of anyone at this table is not worth Brand." She was looking at Adam as she finished her speech.

Everyone was affected by her words. Knowing how smart she was and letting each word sink in, the discussion of finding Brand Wright was over.

Dragonfly then said, "I think Captain Jones will agree that even without our help, Brand may come back on his own. He is a hard man to kill." She was looking at Sam Smith when she said it.

Sam Smith looked a bit ashamed. "She's right."

A ship arrived the next morning for Sam Smith, who was now heading to Earth. This time, Adam and Jayne were also going with him. Jayne no longer had any connection to the Nevermore. On top of that, she had never seen Earth.

It was a new beginning for her, and with that excitement, she was eager to explore a different life. After her latest adventures and using introspection, she was not who she was. Now, her life was with Adam, her beloved.

Utago ship moved merchandise around the galaxy while also answering all distress calls. His time alone in the tube had affected him more than he ever let on. His people admired and loved him.

Dragonfly and Bubba were going to travel the galaxy but only as tourists. Interfering in any local or other matters that did not directly involve them was off-limits. They had developed deep feelings for each other, both casualties of loneliness with real respect and love for each other's wellbeing.

PART 2

18

YOU DON'T KNOW

The Core had successfully infiltrated the Nevermore and brought its destruction from within. After so many years of trying to blow it up, the old methods still worked best. Once you have people on the inside, especially near the top of the command structure creating mayhem, the end will follow.

Then, they were able to get Plutoneus' time capsule to complete their plan of a public execution. Still, they wanted him to be really alive while this was done. Not faked in any way. The whole point was to prove their dominance. It would be a very special execution that the galaxy would remember for quite some time.

Being the biggest business in the galaxy, the Galaxy Corporation was aware of many new and strange events within their galaxy. One was a group of travelers that had traveled from galaxies far away. Their sciences and technologies were greatly more advanced than Galaxy Corporation had ever seen.

In one example, they had taken a picture by a seashore. It looked perfectly flat, like an ordinary picture on Earth. They had people hold and shake the picture by the edges, but nothing happened.

Then, they had a person put their finger in the sand in the picture, and the sand came out onto his hand as if he were there. They used a small vile and scooped some water in the picture. Under microscopes, there were microscopic creatures living in the water. Somehow, they had captured static and dynamic action at the same time. You could feel the heat when inserting a finger into the picture.

There were many new impressive wonders they had, yet the most important to the Core was their life regenerator machine. They decided to use it on Plutoneus, and if it worked, then it would be stored and used only by very important people.

All the travelers wanted were some very unique elements that could only be found or created within this galaxy. Some were very rare, but nothing that really would cost the Core very much. It appeared too good to be true.

The regenerator, as it was referred to, had taken six weeks to finish the job on Brand. It was amazing how it perfectly fixed each part that was injured. It did this while keeping Brand immobilized during the entire procedure. He had lasted the 23 seconds it had taken to transfer him to the device.

Once in there, it appeared time had stopped while he was being repaired. The end result was that he not only was physically fixed but also retained all of his memories. Later, it was learned that his mind was always active the whole time, even while he was in the time capsule. This was achieved by the chip that was given to him by The First People.

———

The adage, "Be careful what you wish for," was never truer for the Core. They now had a fully functioning Plutoneus ready for their supreme execution. Unfortunately, he came with very bad news.

The Core had summoned Brand to feel his fear, to show him that no one was more powerful than the Galaxy Corporation, to humiliate him and feel the satisfaction of a defeated enemy below them.

He was brought into a room that had an elevated floor so that the Core was four feet higher than the floor surrounding them. There were guards surrounding him, but he was no real threat. Weaponless and old, he could not do much to harm anyone in the room.

Not knowing any of the speakers who addressed him, in his mind, he numbered those who talked for his internal review later.

Brand was told about his special execution in great detail, including how painful and long it would last. At that point, he was asked what his thoughts were regarding that.

The weird feeling in the room was how relaxed Brand was. Many people were not afraid to die, yet no one wanted it to be a painfully long experience. Their words had no effect on his outside expressions.

Speaker one, "Are you too scared to speak? I imagine you to be much greater than this."

Speaker two, "He was never great, just lucky. We have destroyed the Nevermore from the inside. What are your thoughts on that?"

More speakers were throwing taunts and insults that had no effect.

Finally, Brand looked at the group above him with a cocky grin as he began to address them.

"You don't know, do you?" He waited a few seconds and continued. "None of you have any idea." With that, he could not help but laugh. It started slow but started to overtake his body, with uncontrollable laughter.

Speaker one, "His mind has broken. The regenerator is flawed, this reaction was not predicted."

Brand now woke up in action with his words. "I will first tell you about your doom and then how I know about it. After that, I will tell you how we might all have a chance of avoiding it. Of course, most will die in that fight, including myself."

Then began a loud argument amongst the Core on whether to entertain any more of Plutoneus' nonsense or just have him removed and out of sight until the execution. It went on for quite some time, with voices becoming very loud.

Some were showing intense emotions, which was a sign of how deeply he had affected them. Brand was patient, enjoying their discord, but after a while, he began again.

"The doom that is coming will destroy this entire galaxy. It is a force that cannot be imagined. They outnumber us by 1,000 to 1 for every being that lives here. Their power is far above blowing up planets as they can detonate suns to go supernova. Their intelligence is greater than most living in the universe, yet what is worse is their hatred directed towards us!"

He looked at the beings above him to gauge if his words had any effect on whether they were now interested in his message. Their silence and intent stares answered that question, so he continued.

"They hate me the most, which we can use to our advantage, but others did help me, and they are not going to pick and choose. They decided our galaxy would be used as an example to others that they were back and in control."

Now, speaker two angrily asked, "Who is this great enemy that we are supposed to be scared of? You're pathetic in your attempt to save your life!"

That touched a nerve, and Brand's attitude totally changed.

"You think I am trying to save my life? You are the idiots that brought me back. I did not ask for that. In my former state, they could not hurt me. If you interrupt me again, I will keep my knowledge, and you all will suffer greatly."

Brand now said nothing. He just looked at the group and dared them to say a word. After 10 seconds, which felt much longer, he continued, with an attitude of trying to help them.

"I will tell you your enemy. I am sure some of you know about them. What you don't know is their new breakthrough in travel. Get ready to meet, as they are saying, your new lords, The First People!"

Complete silence was heard after that. It was like the lack of sound was a sound within itself. Something that could not only be heard but felt like a presence residing in the room.

A speaker Brand had not heard before began to talk. The voice sounded like a scientist with skepticism yet wanting answers.

"How could you know what you are saying? Also, The First People have not been active in the present universe except for their ships when found."

Brand now playing to his audience, responding with courtesy and encouragement.

"Thank you for that good question. I will be glad to explain all I know. This problem is much bigger than anyone here. All our families, friends, and acquaintances will face peril if we do not act wisely. To completely answer your question, I will start from the beginning."

Brand would periodically stop to study the faces of the group that made the Core. He always believed unless you really have someone's attention when speaking, you are just wasting your time. They were all looking at him except for one member.

He continued, "This problem started when I went to Antarctica to investigate a pyramid under the ice. I met The First People's android, which gifted me with what I thought was a communication chip that had implanted itself within my brain.

The chip did do all translations of languages but so much more. A human brain is really two brains in one skull. Each brain works at a different frequency. When you can combine both sides to a mutual frequency, the real power of the brain is unleashed.

The chip inside my head does that for me without the need for meditation or any substances. Once a human brain is synced, galactic knowledge is available regarding most questions.

Time does not exist within this thought mode, as time and space have no bearing on thoughts. They can exist outside those constructs. Also, what is known as quantum entanglement is abundant, letting The First People know what happened here in real time where they currently are located."

Brand could tell he needed to give them proof or at least something very real for them to think about.

Brand's tone now had concern within it. "I have information that you may want to keep confidential. I suggest that everyone besides the Core leave the room before I continue."

Again, there was a discussion amongst the group, with the first speaker ordering all others out of the room.

For Brand, that was a victory. His nature was to control the situation, even if it was his death to come. He felt more powerful, which fed upon itself.

"You have all been played." Looking at the group, he changed his words.

"You have been used for someone else's benefit. They had taken advantage of your greed while figuring that you would use it to kill your enemy, me. Who do you think sent the Travelers? They are a race working with The First People. Via the nature of their bodies, they can move incredibly quickly in space. They collected some of their technologies and brought them to you. Knowing you could not resist and figuring you would do exactly what you have done."

Brand had now given them the kicker. Very few knew about the Travelers, and he now had them where he wanted. They were most receptive to the following announcement.

"The First People have developed the ability to travel anywhere within the Universe almost instantly, and it gets worse."

Each Core member's face was staring at Brand, some with concerned looks while others trying to figure out a solution. Only one seemed not interested. Now was the time to give them his plan while he really had their focus. He was feeling good, and his tendency to talk in riddles began.

"Do you have a lottery here? On Earth, they do. The chance of winning is very slim, yet if you don't play, the chance of losing is guaranteed."

Usually, Brand would see if the recipient could figure out what he is saying, wait for a reply, and if there is none, then go into what he meant. This time, there was no room for fooling around. He continued without a pause.

"I am your lottery ticket. Without me, you will lose. Even with my help, the chances are greatly against us. Our enemy has few weaknesses, yet there are some. Using their hatred for me against them is one of them."

Checking on his audience, making sure he still had their complete attention, Brand continued.

"They will be here before you execute me. If they wanted, they could be right here on this planet in under three minutes. I have a plan. Please listen, realize how much is at stake, and think of all you have to lose before you give me your answer. Also, realize that time is something none of us have. Each moment you linger in your decision, our chances of survival lowers."

Brand then went over his plan, including most of the details. Of course, he left things out, always trying to have a few surprises in his arsenal when needed.

Before they provided their answer, the member who never paid attention to Brand's speech addressed him.

"Plutoneus, you may have fooled my associates, but make no mistake, I don't believe a word you have spoken. Your nature is to double-cross all you encounter. We did not just fix you. A very powerful bomb has been implanted in you and can be detonated at any time. I figure you will try to escape once the fighting, if there is any, begins. Or at least when so many fighters are grouped together, thinking they might save you. It will only take an instant to explode you in a million pieces."

With that, he smiled, looking right into Brand's eyes.

Brand replied to his smile with an evil smile, like a grin when you know you have beaten your enemy and responded.

"Well, you would be doing me a great favor. I either have to look forward to a long, slow, painful execution by the Core or an even worse fate by The First People. Do you think you scare me with your current words? Hit the button now. Destroy your only hope. I dare you!"

The first speaker now interjected quickly with, "We have made our decision and will follow your advice. Now, we will work on your plan. You will have a guard detail but will be treated as a guest until either this event occurs, or your execution date arrives.

The meeting was over for now, but the final battle was just beginning. There was a word from a planet that sounds like *oleapol*, meaning the beginning and ending happening at the same time. The contradiction is built into its meaning. Used to describe an almost impossible situation.

The *oleapol* was happening, starting slowly yet building upon itself. Soon, a plan would go into effect, that would seem futile. The future is very different than the past and present. It is just a bunch of probabilities, with some having very high chances of happening. Even with that, what will actually happen can also be a very low chance, just with much higher odds of probabilities against it. The bottom line was no one really can know until it was revealed in the present.

Funny how you can feel good even knowing that pending doom is at your doorstep. Brand now was in a very nice room and had his privacy. That feature of existence cannot be overrated. It is taken for granted when had and longed for so greatly when denied.

Having his privacy felt so good, during his sleep he never felt like he had it. Being solely in a dream state was the problem. Now that he was awake, he could step out of the Galactic Information Service and have a sense of a private self.

There also was a freedom to know that whatever happens, the continual existence of life was not an option. So much of the present was used for surviving in the future, and when that did not exist, a new freedom is found.

19

THE CALL

The beginning of the plan is picking a planet to make their *oleapol.*

There are some events that happen within the galaxy that are so dramatic that everyone who hears them can tell you where they were, what they were doing, and who they were with.

Time has no effect as it is burned into the memory, whether young, old, or in between. Binding so many different beings with a similar memory. Like a marker in history, things will always be what they were before and after that event.

It went out on a million different channels in all different forms that were used in communications. Never had the galaxy heard the same message at the same time with such a large audience. No matter who you spoke with, they also heard and were affected by it.

"To all who hear this message, I am back. Most know me as Plutoneus. My name is not important. My message is vital. We are under attack today, tonight, and tomorrow. We are just one people fighting an enemy that will destroy all we love. All disputes between everyone and every planet or organization must be suspended until we win this war. I need warriors, people willing to fight and die to save us all. Our enemy outnumbers us and will give no mercy in our dispatch. I need warriors from every planet who are willing to fight for their planet, their galaxy, and their loved ones. I will be leading this battle and willing to die with honor for it. All warriors come immediately to planet Fattalla, also known as Q2D13S4891P8."

The message was repeated continuously for the next three days.

It was unknown what response the galaxy would provide. When creating a new moment that has never been experienced before, who can truly predict? Part of Brand's plan needed the scope and power only the Core could provide.

He instructed the Core that they would need thousands of people doing all different tasks, which would need to be in place instantly. Even to Brand, it felt like an impossible request that only people who truly believed him would try to conquer.

One of the tasks was that everyone who joined their army needed to be completely documented individually and fully identified. Their names, pictures, life story, and what led them to The Final Battle, as it was now being referred to.

Also, each person must be a volunteer who is doing this solely of their own accord.

Brand had promised that all who joined would never be forgotten. Whatever happens in The Final Battle, all would be remembered and honored for their efforts.

What happened next surprised everyone, wondering how many thousands would answer the call. It wasn't thousands, it was millions. From everywhere in the galaxy, places known and others never heard of.

Not only did the galaxy send warriors, but supplies came pouring in, and there were all different things that might be useful. Sent with no charge, some with entities on how to use the equipment sent.

Clothes, food, weapons, medical supplies, and so many other gifts were given. If the Core had doubts about Brand's story, the galaxy believed Plutoneus fully.

Even more than what was sent was what was happening within the galaxy. Wars that had lasted between planets for centuries paused. Almost all fighting had stopped, as everyone now had a common enemy and purpose in survival.

Never had the galaxy had a singular purpose and cause for survival. In an unfortunate way, it was beautiful, and it was marvelous to see everyone get along and work on a project for all.

Brand had less than three weeks before the Core's execution would occur. Time was moving so fast with so many decisions to be made that he had little time to think about others in his past life. That is how it now felt to him. All that had happened before was exactly that. This was the only reality he had. Only what was included in it, did he contemplate.

When King Utago heard the broadcast, which was now known as The Call, he was amazed at how Brand kept coming back into the picture. He had maintained good communication with both Jayne and Bubba. He knew they had nothing to do with Brand's resurrection, which made it that much more amazing.

His first thought was, of course, that he would join The Final Battle. There was no more noble cause, regardless of the outcome. Yet now he was a King, if he had been a captain, it would have been different.

His crew was not really a crew but his people. They had put not just their lives in his care with complete faith. It was more than that. They had personally chosen him to be their King. It was more than a word but a true change in a person's perspectives and actions. Kings do not abandon their subjects.

Whether The Final Battle is won or lost, he will always be one who did not participate, and that will haunt him until his death. There was more than his personal happiness now that he was King. His family, as he thought of them, always came first.

They begged him not to go, knowing he would want to be there.

He agreed and, in the end, became a shuttle service for those who wanted to join. Everyone in the galaxy who was in the know was either participating in the battle or doing some service to benefit that cause.

Jayne thought about when she first met Utago and her apprehension about trusting him. How things had changed, his periodic contact became her only news regarding galactic events. She now trusted not only his information but his judgment.

Utago had recorded The Call and played it for Jayne. They were using a video connection, which allowed Utago to register Jayne's physical reaction to the news. It reminded him of someone obsessed with faith in something which was now proven true.

Her body had frozen so as not to miss a word or sight that was being shown.

"I knew he would be back. I must join him in this. I feel like I was born for this moment, that there is some further part that needs to be performed. Please, King Utago, please take me to him."

Utago, since becoming King, had to involve himself in what others would call awkward situations. Most do not understand the downside of the title. It appears like the greatest thing someone could want, and it is until they have it.

Between the politics and those seeking your position, there are the boring ceremonies to contend with. Also, they have to make decisions that affect people's personal lives. Now, King Utago was fighting an internal conflict about whether he should bring up Adam since he was not mentioned.

"Dear Jayne, it is not a problem to honor your request. Is Adam joining you?"

"I love him so much, yet this life is not my destiny. If I tell him he will want to join us, and his life is too precious. This life I now live is too easy and feels wrong. My whole life was about the war, dedication, and doing without. I don't want Adam getting hurt."

Utago, now King, responded, "By leaving Adam, he will be worse than hurt."

Jayne's anger quickly rose, "Will you take me or not!"

"Of course. Be ready in 14 hours. I will contact you for pickup."

Jayne, now feeling sad in many different ways, said, "Sorry, King Utago, for-"

"No sorry needed. Life is filled with hard choices. I, too, greatly want to join The Final Battle, and will forever regret not being there. We all have our reasons. I look forward to seeing you again."

With that, the transmission ended with both participants being in a melancholy state.

Jayne had to now deal with her choice, a decision that would forever change not just her life but also the man she loved. She thought, *Why do things always have to be so hard, with actions making the road not taken forever remain in a person's heart?*

Now, with just 14 hours till a new life's journey began, she could not bear to tell Adam to his face. She had not thought about where King Utago would land to retrieve her. Her mind was racing with thoughts and plans, plus the guilt of knowing what she was going to do.

She thought that this situation was worse than when she was imprisoned in Gentry's home. The thought that she could still change her mind came and went quickly. Jayne contacted King Utago to set up where and how the pickup would take place. Being in a relatively desolate area, now the real hardship began. What words would she find to use in her video text to explain to Adam why she must go, and he must stay.

———

They both heard The Call together. Captain Jones first spoke about it.

"That man is indestructible. I just knew in my heart that he would be back, we must go!"

Dragonfly's love for Bubba was her first affection for anyone and her greatest pleasure. They had been having a wonderful time, and she figured Brand would extinguish that.

She replied, "Of course, we will, but as we have promised each other, there will be no involvement besides a brief visit for moral support." She was giving Bubba her sweetest smile, and her voice had a sweet tone to it.

The truth was Bubba did not want to be involved in this conflict. He also enjoyed his time with Dragonfly, and it reminded him of being a child. With that, he thought, *why is it that when we are children, all we want is to be adults? Then, as adults, we desire to be as happy and free as children.*

Now, he would have to leave that wonderful feeling of being a child to become an adult again. The feeling was bittersweet.

He asked her, "What is he referring to? Can you do anything to help without getting too involved?" As he asked her, he also thought about how Brand always got involved in trouble.

"It is with people you have some experience with. And yes, I am working on something."

Now Bubba gave her the look to provide the information.

She continued, "It is The First People." As she said that for the first time, she saw fear in her Bubba's face.

Dragonfly continued, "What I am working on cannot be talked about!" With that, she gave the look of this conversation is over. They agreed to see Brand one last time, making it very brief.

So many beings answered The Call. Whatever was going to happen, their courage to fight for everyone else's survival shined.

The Core was planning all contentions, half the group thought it was a bluff and were trying to figure out how best to profit once the event never happened. They had decided that either way, if it did occur and somehow Plutoneus survived, or it never took place, they would kill him in a much more private setting.

The other half were much more worried about the threat than anything else.

Never will the stories of all who participated get told, yet one volunteer to The Final Battle called herself Cake. It really was a nickname she was given, and she liked it so much that it became her title from then on.

Cake had a human form and, if seen on Earth, would look she was in her upper twenties with long black hair, she weighed around 200 pounds on a frame of five feet and five inches. She had a wonderful spirit with an abundance of energy.

During her orientation, it was revealed that she did not want to kill anyone yet and also wanted to be on the battlefield. Her desire was to help the brave soldiers defending our galaxy with ammunition and food. She had no children of her own but had many brothers and sisters within her family. She told them her plans to help in The Final Battle, and they were proud of her decision.

Her story was recorded per orientation instructions. She was assigned to a unit and was now waiting for orders.

It felt amazing how many answered The Call. All different types of beings from all different planets and races. Some from business and scientific backgrounds, which would not have been expected, volunteered for the type of carnage that was to come.

There were rejections based on certain factors, such as age or mental fitness, etc. Also, there were rejections regarding the reasons why some wanted to fight.

Their ranks grew quickly, everyone having high spirits, feeling the power and strength they had in numbers and the commitment to the cause.

By this point, Brand was being treated more like the commanding general than a prisoner soon to die by the people he was fighting to save.

At times, he had what was called the dead stare. It has been referred to by many other names. It is when someone has seen so much death their eyes become blank, empty of emotion or thought. It is an uncomfortable feeling to observe. During his stay in the time capsule, he observed many different versions of the future, which affected him.

It was said that at times, he was so funny or animated on some fact while at other moments a person in deep mourning. Periods where he said nothing but had his dead stare and, other times, visiting as many warriors as possible that he could meet. Thanking everyone while taking pictures of themselves together. He spoke about how proud and honored he was to serve with them and how they would never be forgotten. On that last point, he promised to all he encountered.

There were other beings that were there strictly on their own terms. The truth was all who helped in any way they chose was beneficial.

What was amazing was how fast and many all responded. Not only did millions respond, but that was just in the first couple of days.

20

MANNY

Brand knew their time was short. He only had eight days before his execution. He had no doubt The First People would arrive before then. Just how much before then? Also, he had seen many variations of the conflict to come. Now, it felt like he was talking to ghosts. People who were only going to exist for a short time before death caught up. So much life will soon to be gone forever.

He thought about time, which was an area that always amazed Brand. In the past, he had experienced time slowing down. It was the concept of time that got to him. An invisible thing that moved at different speeds depending on different events. This thing ran almost all the lives it encountered. It not just ran but controlled their lives and was still very hard to define.

Time was now on his mind like most of his life, controlling his thoughts and actions. *Maybe that is why days off are so nice,* he thought. He would put time aside and live without the constraints of eating or sleeping at specified times of the day or night.

His primary guard had a very long name, which Brand renamed him to "Manny." He had hair with black curls that draped around his head, which was offset against his big smile and sharp perception, making him hard to miss.

It did not take long before Manny changed from his guard to being his top general. The two instantly respected each other when they met. Unlike Utago, who was impressed with Brand's boldness and fearlessness, Manny found it to be his knowledge of so many things plus Brand's swagger.

To Brand, all the people from his past life were missing, and his end was soon to come. These people around him, warriors, guards, generals, whatever title they had, were his family now.

It was not that he had forgotten those from his past, but these souls were standing right now with him at his end. Even more than that, they were putting their lives on the line, chancing all their precious time!

Today, Manny and Brand were going over the battlefield, using different strategies depending on how the unknown would reveal itself.

Fattalla had beautiful fields surrounded by mountains. They were huge and flat with a greenish-pink color on the surface. It was a type of spongy grass that had more bounce than grass on Earth. Yet it was super soft to the touch.

On one side of the field to their left, as they had taken one side, figuring their enemy would take the other side. This was ordered by Brand. At times, it was like he was reliving the event before it happened.

The left side had a forest-type feature. It looked like bamboo trees, making fighting within that area very tight.

To the right was a pond that traveled past the horizon. The water was deep, giving it an unwelcome feeling, its temperature being cold, thus making it a wall in that direction.

Brand had given Manny a list of names that, if any arrived, he would be notified of it immediately.

The planet had three suns, making night almost impossible. There were periods when it became darker, feeling like an overcast day, but mostly it was sunny. At times, it would become hot when the suns were close together and above them.

They were setting up supply stations every two miles deep and long until they reached the middle of the field. If looked at from above, it became a grid of small shacks aligned equally, filling half the rectangle it occupied.

The stations were equipped with food and ammunition, plus medical supplies. There was also a piece of communication equipment within each station that could contact other stations, plus their command center.

When Manny spoke to Brand, unfortunately, he was in his dead stare.

"Boss, one on your special list has contacted us and wants a sit-down. He has a guest who is not on the list but insists she must also be granted equal access to the meeting. Before you ask, his name is King Utago, and the guest is Jayne Stillwater. I assume you want to see them, so I have arraigned it-"

Now he did some calculations and continued, "-one hour from now." With that, a big smile appeared on his face.

Brand was still thinking within himself. The dead stare had ended with internal thoughts now taking the stage. Still, no response was given to Manny.

Manny continued, "It will be good for you to see some old friends. It is set up in the blue room. The communications will be tested in…six hours." With that, he went over to inspect other operations. Manny was like that, always moving while really seeing. Watching and moving, directing while using his shirt communicator.

Brand was thinking about how quickly Utago had become King. He had been a ship captain, but that is nothing compared to being King. It amused him with all that was going on, he would feel jealous of that. His death should be a concern, yet the fact that Utago became King made him laugh.

The best laugh one can have is when it is directed at ourselves. He hadn't laughed like that in so long. It was like long lost food the body desperately needed and had just found. To say it felt good would truly not express the joy he was feeling at that moment. He wanted to live so he could be a king like Utago.

Even Manny had stopped at the sight. There was Plutoneus in uncontrollable laughter.

21

LAST MEETING

As hard as he could try, nothing came to mind with the name Jayne Stillwater. That did not surprise him, as he would leave a bigger impression on others than they did on him. Now, being old and having so many acquaintances, much had become blurred.

He was excited to see King Utago and made a special note to himself to be sure to use his title when addressing him. He still was trying to place Jayne, hoping it would come once he saw her face.

Brand was sitting in the blue room, which was a temporary tent-like structure with different room functions. One is an informal conference-type setting. There were big pillow-type seats that could take different forms depending on the controls located on them. It was called the blue room from the outside color of the structure, having a blueish shade.

Even though Brand was a prisoner technically, not only did he not have guards watching him, but also no guards defending him. He moved about just like everyone else there, no special treatment given.

Yes, he did give orders, but they were just about winning The Final Battle. So, he was surprised when Utago made his entrance.

There were his guards numbering eight, with two personal assistants to finish the procession. His four soldiers entered the room first, then Utago and Jayne, with an assistant at each side, respectively.

Finishing were the last four guards, all with serious faces, looking like they expected The Final Battle to begin in minutes.

Brand jumped up from the chair and moved toward Utago and Jayne. His guards quickly looked at their King and then relaxed as he nodded it was okay.

"King Utago, it is wonderful seeing you again. I can't wait to hear all about your adventures and becoming a King!" Brand had said that with a big smile and hand outstretched in greeting."

"I am glad to see you are back to your old self. Jayne Stillwater, from the Nevermore, has put her life in danger trying to save your life." With that, Utago had stopped with Brand, now understanding his mistake.

Now, applying his full attention to Jayne and looking at her with utmost importance, he addressed her.

"Dear Jayne Stillwater, it is an honor to meet you at this time. Thank you for your actions, which I want to hear all about, every detail." Then he opened his arms, and Jayne and Brand hugged for the first time.

Brand then continued, "Now I know you both can't stay here long, so we must use what little time we have enjoying old moments and hearing new stories."

Utago, putting his head down a bit, said, "I will not be joining you at this battle. Jayne has chosen to stay and fight by your side."

Brand's mood instantly changed from happy to serious, saying the following.

"Utago, you are a King and have your people to care for. That is your only choice. And for you, young lady, it is my honor to have you by my side. Now we will have a fancy meal, and I will listen to all your adventures."

Jayne was beaming, like when your imagination cannot create a scenario that is as great as the events that are happening right now to her. She felt like her whole existence was for this moment, this event, and making it even better being with her hero.

To people not committed to a cause they love, the dream of helping others while risking certain death would seem crazy to be happy in doing it. Jayne was not that different than the millions of others who had joined, having love for people they know and don't know, willing to give all for the many.

With so much bad that was in the galaxy, it was hard to remember how much good there also was. On the planet, Fattalla was the biggest collection of beings willing to sacrifice their lives for something greater than their own.

As fate would have it, Manny interrupted Brand with the news that two others on his list had arrived.

"Boss, Captain Jones, and Dragonfly have arrived. They seek your company. What would you like done?"

Brand's happiness could not be hidden. He lit up, and there was a glow on his face, and his back straightened.

"Perfect timing. We are going to have a banquet for Jayne and King Utago. It will be at the Grove, love that place. Have Captain Jones and Dragonfly meet us there."

Brand then realized that Bubba now also had a title. So much had changed while he was in his time capsule. His mind wondered how all these changes had happened. He felt his relationship with Bubba would never be the same as it was.

Then, thoughts of how lucky he was to have all his friends with him one last time. Deep down, he wished Jayne would not follow in this fight, yet it was for each to make their own decision. She was special. He could tell by the impression she had made on Utago.

At that moment, he decided to keep her by his side for as long as time would allow to find out as much as he could about her life and past adventures.

Brand's gut feeling was that neither Bubba nor Dragonfly were going to help in the battle that was coming. Yet there was also something that he could not define in the back of his mind, associated with Dragonfly and The Final Battle.

Whatever happened, it was fate that they would all be together again that day. He knew that, except for Jayne, it would be the last time he would ever see them.

The Grove was a beautiful little spot surrounded by trees and many different types of flowers. It had a vibration of peace, and Brand had instantly fallen in love with that spot. There were tables created from rocks that were polished to a high degree and felt so right with the environment. They also had rock benches that were not connected to the tables but worked well with them. Whatever the rock was made of, it was strong but not heavy enough to hinder moving them around.

There were people handling all types of work that did not involve fighting. They had come to help in ways they could, in this case, setting up a feast for Plutoneus and his friends.

King Utago, plus his party with Jayne and Brand, arrived at the Grove just before Captain Jones and Dragonfly showed up.

They had sat down at a long rectangular table, with Brand at one end and Jayne sitting on his right side. Maybe it was the loving vibrations Jayne was giving Brand, for in his short time with her, he had a great desire to protect her. Thus, he wanted to keep her close. He used to tell people in charge to keep their eyes on the prize.

Brand could tell she was extraordinary, someone who made special things happen. He decided to guard her for as long as he lived or until at least this event was over. Deep down, he knew she would not leave as long as he stayed, and his leaving was impossible.

Captain Jones and Dragonfly were walking side by side. They were not holding hands, but you could tell they treated each other as equals. More than that, their feelings for each other were apparent without words.

When Brand first saw Bubba, he slowly rose from his bench, hardly walking. Like he was frozen for the moment, in deep thought, after a few seconds, he was back moving at normal speed toward his old friend.

They hugged, and then, while Brand was acknowledging Dragonfly, Jayne followed him and gave Bubba a big hug. Brand could tell that she also had made a big impression on Bubba. She discreetly handed Bubba something, which he quickly pocketed.

There was a special look between Utago and Dragonfly, and they showed respect for each other's position and accomplishments.

Dragonfly said while making a show of it, "Congratulations, King Utago, on all your achievements in such a brief period of time. Amazing and well deserved!"

Now Utago responded to his former boss, "Being around you, my Queen, was the inspiration to achieve great deeds."

Brand could stand no longer not knowing the full stories of each. They all sat down with Jayne, who was still on Brand's right side. Then, taking turns, each provided their stories while together and then separated from each other.

All were happy, but sadness was creeping into Brand's heart. Now, feeling guilty about how much each person there had risked for his benefit. Changing each at the table, with a mixture of positive and negative results.

King Utago asked Brand, "When do you expect the attack to begin?"

"Definitely before my execution." Brand had a big smile and continued more seriously, "Soon, maybe after three or four days. Any time from then. It will start quickly, and that is why we are currently living around our side of the field, to be ready!"

Brand continued, "I so appreciate your visit, but I will request you all leave by tomorrow. Of course, except for Jayne."

Then, looking at her, he said, "And it's never too late to change your mind. You have already done so much." Shifting his attention to the group stated.

"I would like to speak with Dragonfly in private before you leave."

Dragonfly answered, "I also wanted to speak privately with you. How about later, before we retire for the night?"

Brand responded, "Perfect!"

The scene that night of the battlefield was surrounded by so many groups of different types of people, their morale was high. If you did not know why they were all gathered together, you might think it was some big positive event and they were there to get front row seats.

There were all different types and styles of lights that spread across the area. All types of music and talk could be heard. Even laughter came through the background of sounds in certain spots.

Brand was sitting on a slope that was almost the center of the main battlefield. There were three other fields adjacent that were set up for battle. Looking over all the lights and sounds, his emotions felt like they were on a roller coaster ride.

One moment, knowing that unless something changes, this will all be for nothing. The next was so proud of all around him, their courage and their willingness to stand up for something that might cost them everything. He wondered if he would have answered that call.

He started to drift off into his dead stare when Dragonfly came up behind him.

"Do you ever just want to run away, disappear from the galaxy, or are you looking forward to dying this way? Look how many are now involved because of you."

Brand answered with his dead stare intact, "They are all volunteers. And yes, I would love to be left alone. Of course, that was with Sweetbull, who is no longer with me. I feel there is a chance, and somehow it involves you!"

Now, he turned around and looked into Dragonfly's eyes. "I can see many things in my head that I should not know. Yet there are certain things that are locked up, blind to my eyes and thoughts. Yes, I know about your time crystals and would like you to create me a body shield utilizing their energy and also a weapon that will be attached to my hand using that energy. But there is more. I do not know your final place within all this, yet I know it will come. Do the right thing!"

Dragonfly, now smiling, changed her attitude, "Don't I always do the right thing?" Laughing to herself, she continued.

"Have you been using your RB abilities on me? I already have created what you want, it was going to be a surprise. Just figured you could use it. I want to add a chip inside you to operate it-"

Brand now interrupted her, "Not needed. I will be able to connect and operate it from the chip already inside my head from The First People. It is amazing all the things that chip can do."

Dragonfly looked at him questionably, "What if they turn it off once they get here? Then your weapon will be useless."

Brand looked at her, thinking that is the problem when you think you are the smartest in the room. Not everything makes logical sense.

He began, "Of course, you are right if all they wanted to do was defeat and kill me. Their society has changed again. Now, they want expansion and domination. Sure, there are easier and safer ways for them to accomplish their mission. But that would be missing the point. Even though they will slaughter us, they have their own honor code. There would be no honor in doing it the way you suggested. We, even you, fear death, so it controls us. They care not about death but glory. Imagine the most ruthless warriors who are also incredibly smart, agile, strong, and can work as a team. This whole event to them is just the beginning of the fun they will bring to this galaxy."

Dragonfly said nothing at first but then, "So what is all this for?" She moved her right arm, pointing from one end of the battlefield to the opposite side.

Brand, who had never taken his eyes off her and showed no emotion or energy, replied with four words.

"Do the right thing!"

Then, asking her where his new weapon and shield were located,

Dragonfly provided Brand with his new equipment. She was in deep thought about whether Brand knew her plan and what he thought was the right thing. Nothing more about it was spoken.

22

PIERCE AND ADAM

When Adam saw the video left for him by Jayne, the mixture of emotions became overwhelming. Anger, fear for Jayne, sorrow for himself, with the feeling that what he must do needed to be done right now.

He had moved to DC because of his time with Sam Smith. Adam enjoyed his company and being close to someone who was powerful had his own allure. Now, he was the perfect person to contact, someone who could actually make what Adam wanted, happen. He had his personal phone number and called.

Sam, who was usually short with words, saw Adam was calling, and he answered, saying, "Yes?"

"Hello Sam, this is Adam. You have to help me, I need to go to Fattalla, that's a planet-"

"I am aware of that planet. I will send a car to pick you up, and we can talk in my office, okay?"

"Yeah, that sounds great, thanks. You're going to send it right now, right?"

"Yes." Then Adam heard the line go dead.

Sam Smith had been thinking prior to his call that once Adam did his first kill, he really would be ready for some dangerous missions. Sam was impressed with Adam during their LaTaFree trip. He might

153

even be better than Brand Wright, yet some people would rather be killed than actually kill someone. Adam had not graduated in that area, as Sam Smith liked to think about it.

He did not want to take him to The Final Battle. Then again, Sam also wanted to be there, not to fight but to be close to the action. He felt this was his fate, having Adam tip the scales into his going, and now both of them to journey off together.

Sam instructed his driver to take Adam up to his office via the back entrance. There was much less security and only one physical person to deal with. It was his secretive nature not wanting documentation of this meeting. He contacted the guard and instructed him not to record anything.

Sam's office had an office connected to it that could be accessed by the back entrance. It was used when Sam had to remove certain people from his office to never be seen again in this world. They came in the front door and then were removed via his back office.

Adam arrived at Sam's office from his back office doorway.

"Hello Sam, thanks so much for hearing me out. She's left. Jayne went to fight in the Final Battle. I want to go there and be by her side. I know you can make that happen!"

Sam, without emotion, responded, "If you go, you will most likely die. I imagine that does not matter to you. I will personally take you there."

Adam was in shock. He thought it would be so hard to convince him to help. Now that Sam so quickly complied, Adam was at a loss of thoughts for the moment.

"Thank you. How long will it be before we leave?"

"Quickly. Brand's execution is in three days, and the war will start before that."

The knock at Sam's main door interrupted their meeting. To Adam, it felt ominous. He wanted to tell Sam not to open the door. Then, second thoughts came into his head. *This man is doing everything you want, so don't tell him how to live his life.*

Sam ushered Adam into his back office but left the door a bit ajar. He was not sure why he did that. It just felt right, and he was now following his intuition much more.

Sam went back to his chair behind his big old desk and commanded, "Enter."

Pierce walked into the room, yet differently than usual. Sam felt the real Pierce had finally entered his sphere, now wanting to be acknowledged. Pierce walked up to Sam with the desk acting like a wall between them.

As Pierce was looking down at Sam, he slid his hand inside his jacket pocket, pulling out a hypodermic needle and syringe.

Then, saying, "You think you are so smart. Do you know who I am?"

Sam said nothing, not moving a muscle. He just gave an evil stare.

"My name is Pierce, and I am a biological artificial intelligence. The great ones have created me, just one of many different ways we will destroy all humanity on this planet. They have downloaded a portion of their intelligence within a human container, me. It has been wonderful while you have been gone. It is now time to make that permanent."

Pierce was totally focusing on Sam with his back to the door that Adam had now opened. Adam was frozen watching Pierce talking when, in the next moment, Pierce lunged at Sam with the needle heading for his neck. The move was so fast it beat any move Sam had made to block it.

It was sticking in his neck, but the syringe had yet to be pushed. Adam had screamed, "Stop!", which distracted Pierce at the critical moment when he would have pushed the fluid into Sam's bloodstream.

Pierce, not fazed, smiled and said, "You're next. Never liked you!" It appeared he did not take Adam to be any threat and turned back to Sam, who was looking for something within his desk.

Adam looked around the room now with a different feeling within himself. Then, his eye detected a weapon that was close and perfect. Without thought or sympathy for his future victim, he grabbed the spear that was vertically hanging next to the doorway. He ripped it off the wall, feeling no resistance from its former resting place.

Holding it with his left hand in the front and his right hand behind his left, he ran directly at Pierce.

There was no hesitation or any concern for his victim or himself, whether he lived through the event or would be forever punished for it.

Thrusting the spear deeply into Pierce's back, it pushed out his chest, destroying a lung and piercing his heart. Adam kept pushing, and now the spear was 7 inches protruding out of Pierce's chest.

Pierce showed more amazement than pain. It felt like he could not believe Adam had that in him. Now, he was dying. Obviously, he had planned this event many times, but this outcome never happened. As his life was fading, he regained current thoughts, then put his full weight on Sam while grabbing his sides pushed the spear end into Sam's chest.

Adam, now like a hunter, enraged that his prey was still fighting, grabbed Pierce and tossed his body aside. That further damaged Sam's wound, giving him only a few seconds left of life.

Adam looks at Sam with sadness, saying, "I am sorry."

Sam looked back and, with his last breath, said, "Perfect. You're ready!"

————

Colonel Bolt was contacted by a man he had never heard of, yet he knew everything about Bolt. He strongly suggested they meet immediately to resolve a situation. It involved one of his subjects but was much bigger than that.

Bolt, at his age, did not fear death, and his gut feeling was this meeting would change his life. He agreed to meet at a very exclusive restaurant, the kind that almost nobody knew about except for the few that it serviced.

Once there, he was directed to a table with two men already seated. Only one talked, explaining that they were with a group called Delegati. Sam Smith had died and was the current leader. Sam had requested you replaced him. He was highly regarded, and after serious consideration, we agreed.

The way it was communicated, Bolt's decision was already chosen for him. Still, he asked the question.

"What if I refuse this position?"

He answered, "In life and as a soldier, choices will be made for you regardless of your desires. There are incredible perks that come with that position. It is harder to come by than being President. It is your destiny. I don't think you're the kind of man to shrink from your duty when your country and the world need you most."

Bolt knew he was right and was impressed with the ease with which he was answered. These were smart people who knew what they wanted and how to get it.

The man continued, "The first business that needs to be addressed is what you want to be done with Adam Knight. Pierce terminated Sam, and Adam did the same to Pierce. After that, of course, is what is occurring with The Final Battle. Your new title is Senior Advisor to the President. You will have Sam's office and, of course, a pay raise. Congratulations."

With that, both men shook his hand, and it was over.

Bolt's thoughts were racing with all that just transpired, Sam being gone, his new job title, Adam becoming a killer, and Pierce's death. The feeling of immense power of so many things entered his mind.

23

NEW FRIENDS AT THE END

Certain people became close to Brand at the end, Manny plus others. There were the Brothers, as they were usually referred to. Yes, they had individual names but were known just as the Brothers.

They were big, standing over 7 feet tall, mostly with human traits, but did have slight differences. They were so happy and jovial yet dedicated to the cause and Brand's safety.

As soon as Brand had met them, there was an instant bond between the three. Many thought they were his bodyguards.

Then there was Dabs, again, that was not his real name, but the one he had chosen. That was an aspect of all that was there. Each had made that choice of their own free will. True volunteers, in Dabs' case, it was for his girl. They were both young and between the videos and pictures, they were such a beautiful couple with great expectations to come.

Brand believed there was more to it than that, letting that aspect stay in the shadows. He believed we were all trying to prove something, either to ourselves or to the people we love.

Dabs was an example of the best of being young. He had so much energy plus excitement for the future. Brand immediately liked him plus felt bad that he had joined. And that was the way it was for so many Brand had met. Happiness and sadness, an *oleapol* of feelings and events.

Eventually, there were 33 warriors in Brand's personal army, dedicated first to him and then to all else.

Brand had not asked for any of it, yet it felt so good to have people truly on his side. He imagined that was how King Utago must feel, as deep down, he was still jealous of Utago being King.

The time was now closing in as he had less than 48 hours until the Core would execute him.

Jayne was also always by his side. They had spent many hours together, exchanging stories and thoughts about the wonders of the galaxy. Brand easily now understood why she made such a big impression on Bubba and Utago, plus everyone else she met. There was something incredibly special about her. It felt like meeting a superstar before they became famous, yet you knew it will happen. Her bravery was always apparent, yet more than that, it was something that could not be put into words.

Life was such a double-edged sword. This was how Brand had always seen the world, but it was never truer than now. On one side, he wanted Jayne to be as far away from this trouble as could be found. The other side was so happy to get to know her and have her close by him.

It truly was bittersweet feelings that persisted in his mind about so much around him, knowing that so many will die, quite possibly for nothing. *Maybe just all of us getting together for the first and last time, for the grandest oleapol. Bonding in a way that has never happened before or will again,* Brand thought. He could not comprehend the real impact this would have on the galaxy, a bigger transformation than had ever happened before.

More outside races that were operating on their own had arrived. Brand had the feeling that tomorrow would be different than today and all the days before that.

———

Bolt became aware of Adam's desire to be involved in the Final Battle. He was aware of the Jayne connection and also saw Sam's notes regarding Adam's development.

Situations like these are never brought to the Justice Department. There were just too many secrets that would be revealed. In this case, Adam was an asset and would not be charged or hindered in his pursuit of happiness. That is, except for joining Jayne. Bolt had him detained until that affair would be settled. Adam did not know Bolt had given those orders.

Earth was already providing personnel and weapons to that area. There were thousands who volunteered for that mission, only knowing that it was extremely important and very dangerous.

Bolt thought to himself how truly sad it was that so many Americans have no idea how brave and self-sacrificing the women and men who serve in their military were. There was not much more that could be done in time before it was to begin.

His thoughts then went to Subject 9. Everything around that man was incredible. He should not even be alive, yet he still was. Now he was the key focal point in a war to destroy the galaxy. Just unbelievable.

Bolt always had faith in Brand, and that commodity was not unlimited. This time, he felt there was no way he could avoid his fate. He had read most of the files concerning current events, the Core plus The First People.

Talk about being between a rock and a hard place, he thought. He felt his luck had finally run out.

Bolt had known about alien life on Earth, just never realized how many forms plus how populated Earth was with them. Many of them, even the friendly ones, view us as the late arrivals at the party.

Part of the problem with The First People was how little was really known about them. How big will their force be, what weapons will they be using, etc. Currently, all that could be done was watch on the galactic feed that Bolt now had access to.

———

Brand told Manny to get as many of the warriors on the field as possible. To take up the entire field if necessary. Drones would be used to broadcast his voice as he wanted to talk with his warriors. That was always the term he used for the soldiers.

Manny had asked him why he used that word.

"There is power in words. Soldiers fight for their country and money. Warriors are the elite of soldiers who fight for causes. Words matter."

That was why Manny followed and served Brand. He was always impressed with his knowledge.

Morale was high, and there was a great excitement about the broadcast from their leader. Some expected a truly motivational speech, but what they received was not quite that.

Brand was levitating above the ground with the ability to move left, right, up, and down. This was done with a machine using vibrational technology. It was a gift from the Tall Greys. The chip within his head had no problem operating it, which even surprised the Greys.

There was no denying how powerful and wonderful The First People's inventions were.

It was the darkest that the planet Fattalla could produce while it orbited its three suns. There were spotlights coming from two ships highlighting Brand. He did not have a microphone yet, but when he spoke, the sound came out virtually from everywhere.

Brand began with, "Who are we?!"

Then, answering his question with "Warriors!" He began asking the same question over and over again, and the response from the crowd kept getting louder. He asked it ten times, and the last answer was deafening loud.

Now, he acted like he could not hear their answer and asked again, moving his hands to his ears to try and help him hear their response.

It was awesome to hear so many shouting with all their hearts, one single word.

Next, he asks, "Who are we going to kill?!"

With the answer, "The First People!" Again and again, asking, "Who are we going to kill," and hearing the answer, shouted back at him.

Finally looking at his warriors with pride, Brand said the following.

"We will win this battle, this war. Many will die, but our galaxy and loved ones will live because of what happens here. This is the line in the sand, we must hold the line! I am so proud of all that are here. We will win!"

As he spoke those words, he moved over the battlefield and tilted toward his warriors.

Now the question was who would win, with the answer from his warriors being that they would win!

Once it was over, there was a louder tone to the group. They were ready to begin this battle.

Brand had quickly gone into his dead stare after his speech and show. Like he was searching for an answer yet still not seeing the solution.

24

OLEAPOL

A special structure was set up for the command of many different species. Access to that area was strictly prohibited to a select group of beings. Brand had clearance and demanded Manny also have access. After a short time, that was granted.

It was their war room on how to defeat The First People. They had all agreed to have complete control over their own forces while still helping other groups, if possible. Brand explained that, to The First People, this was a test of determination. Which group was stronger, where might makes right. Still, they had their own code of honor. Indiscriminate bombs and weapons like that would not be allowed.

If someone blew up the planet, that would be considered cheating, and not only would they have killed most living there, but in horrible ways. To them, this is like a game that has rules, and cheating has consequences.

There was a feeling by all that the battle would start soon, within hours. A quiet had overtaken the area. Like the calm before the storm, all visitors and people not there for the fight were gone. Only warriors were left with anxious anticipation of what was to come.

There were many command centers on the field, plus on the side of where Brand's forces were located. There was one bigger than all the rest, situated off the biggest field on the side and in the center. It had an observation tower that could support five people at most.

The view was impressive. Currently, Jayne, Brand, and the Brothers' attention were solely focused on it. There were no conversations from anyone, Manny's arrival was visible where the stairs met the floor.

"Guess you are seeing it. What are your orders?"

Manny was referring to the four great ships that had just arrived on their half of the field, forming a semi-circle around it. There was no transition from before to after their arrival. They just popped into existence.

Now Brand, who was sitting, stood up, going to where Manny was located while heading down the stairs.

"How ever many they put onto the field we will do the same."

All could see Manny was troubled by that statement as he asked.

"Don't you think we should have an edge?"

Brand picked up on what he was suggesting and added, "There will be others on our side entering the action that are not technically part of this force."

Brand then thought to himself that he was thinking like The First People, and that's what happens when you really try to get into someone's head. You slowly become them. He wanted it to be a fair fight, to show them we can stand up to them on a level playing field. That they were not afraid to be one on one against them.

The contrasts between the two groups were glaring. The First People had four huge ships equally spaced around their half of the circle. Brand's army was scattered throughout the area in small encampments.

The First People all had uniforms with different colors and designs, designing different ranks or statuses. The group opposed had no uniform or standard weapons. It was a rag-tag of souls, each with the same common purpose.

There were so many differences, yet each group had the same objective: to kill the other. The invaders were not in any particular hurry to depart their ships. They filed out, forming units of fighters in an orderly manner.

As they were forming their battle formations, music had begun playing from their ships. It started with drum beats that became quicker and louder, then the sounds of horns started to fill the air combining with the drums. On top of all that was a voice that sounded almost human, it was harmonizing with all the other sounds, yet also adding feelings to the ensemble.

The music brought energy to everyone who heard it, generating feelings of wanting to battle for a cause.

At first, it looked so small, but then, after two million people were on their side, they started to move slightly forward and stopped.

Brand's side had two million people standing against them. Each side surveyed the other, their enemy.

The First People were large beings averaging 12 feet tall, with very well-defined muscles, having larger heads than humans, and six fingers and toes with a double row of teeth on their upper and lower jaws. They held 6-foot-long swords that had a moving metallic structure while also being able to shoot electric bolts. To finish, they had personal shields for their body armor but no headgear.

A very imposing enemy with their swords bigger than the height of most who opposed them. What was also apparent was how organized they were. Their display of discipline can really make a difference on the battlefield.

For the first time, many others besides Brand now were realizing what they were truly facing, understanding how slim their odds were of survival, let alone defeating The First People.

Brand had his dead stare on, showing no emotions, and commanded the assault to begin. It started slowly, for the line on the field was quite large. The defenders then started to run towards the invaders.

Many on Brand's side stopped short of direct contact, firing their weapons at them instead. The First People started their march towards the other side of the field. The weapon they used was the sword function as they swept through the defenders like a gardener cleaning weeds.

Every now and then, enough firepower would disable their shields, and then, the shots fired would kill one. Yet it was obvious which side was taking greater losses. Now, the odds were 2 to 1 in favor of The First People as they had already killed more than a million of their opponents. It had only been eight hours since the battle began.

It did not take them long as many times they would kill more than one defender with their strong swing and long swords.

There was very little talk coming from the command center where Brand was located.

Brand then said, "Add four million more of our brave warriors to the battle."

With that, many different people were getting on their communicators, telling their subordinates to send in the troops.

The air had changed in sight and smell, now with different smoke screens affecting the field. The taste and smell of blood and body fluids from many different beings permeated the surroundings.

The Reptilians were doing the best against The First People. They had the strength to block the sword attack and use their weapons. They had similar weapons without the moving metallic metal. They were holding their own with almost equal losses on each side.

The Tall Greys were not doing as well as the Reptilians, yet they did provide a fight The First People could not take for granted. There were so many different species fighting them, and that also was a contrast in armies.

The First People were very uniform in style and look. They had distinctive features, but their general appearance was the same height, color, and body type.

Brand was not familiar with many who were also fighting The First People. Even with all their help, their collective group was losing.

Time disappeared in battles like this, and the line broke down into many little battles all along the different parts of the battlefield. Some areas had hills and mountains along the left borders, while there were also lower levels of the field, which were much less desirable.

During all the fighting, people moved or treated the wounded and provided the warriors with food and ammunition. They, too, were being killed quickly and as easily as the people they were trying to care for.

Even with The First People down to 60% of what they started with, they still had not sent more soldiers onto the field.

They seemed to have unlimited energy and quickness. Looking at their faces, they appeared to be enjoying themselves even when wounded. Seeing that on your enemy is very disheartening.

They were clearly better fighters, stronger, bigger, and quicker, plus they had a greater desire to destroy their enemies.

In Brand's mind, the longer the battle lasted, the better chance of some positive outcome. Yet he could take no more watching. He had hoped they would have lasted longer and done better in hurting The First People's onslaught. These were not incriminations against his warriors. He just had hoped it might have turned out somewhat differently.

Brand stated, "It's time." With that, he started to make his way to the battle waging ahead of him. As he moved, his personal army jumped into action, moving as one organism. They were very closely grouped together and, from above, had a different look than the rest of the field. Of course, they would spread out once in battle.

Brand ordered more smoke bombs and moved his group towards the area that looked like bamboo trees on Earth. They weren't bamboo but very similar in features. He had hoped it would hinder The First People's long sword.

His weapon were two laser beams, one coming from each arm. It fitted on his arm, extending 5 inches past his fingers if they were extended. Being on top of his arm and wrist allowed him to use his hands and fingers for other tasks. When his weapon were activated, it could extend to a maximum length of 10 feet or shorter if desired.

The body shield he wore was standard with a modified energy source.

Once on the battlefield, things looked so different from when they were observed from their command position. There, the action did not look real and was easy to define, yet on the ground, there was nothing but chaos and uncertainty.

As the whole galaxy watched, criticism came from everyone about everything. All could see which side was winning, while who's fault for it was yet to be determined. Now, supplies and resources were desperately being directed to that area.

Half of the Core never believed it would happen, while the other members at least knew they had tried, now wishing more should have been done.

There were many suggesting that the planet should be destroyed as that would take care of the problem, not understanding that the fight they were fighting was their only chance of survival.

The First People would blow up stars, not planets, and with quick work, defeat them. This was their test, one chance to see if they could be stopped. To The First People's way of thought, this was a gift to them, eliminating higher types of technology and seeing if they had the will and determination to win with standard weapons.

Very few could get around the blockade surrounding the planet Fattalla. The concern was that someone would try to blow it up or do some other act that would jeopardize everything.

King Utago could only watch what was happening from afar. His sadness extended to the great loss of life, not to the fact that he was not among them. He now wondered why, in the past, he wanted to die like that.

Bubba, looked at Dragonfly and asked, "Are you planning something? They don't look like they have long to go."

She looked back at her first true love, knowing there was only so much she could share with him. Then, for some reason, Sam Smith came into her mind and how he was always short with words.

With a cute smile, "Yes." Then, she left the area to work on just that.

25

THE FINAL BATTLE

Jayne was always near Brand, or maybe he was always near her. It could not be determined. Manny, Dabs, and the Brothers were also always around, along with so many other names. Yet, there was a special connection between Jayne and Brand.

Being in the battle was like nothing you could experience without actually being there. The immediate knowledge that you may die, which was a real possibility, highlighted all the body's senses. Energy becomes abundant, as also uncertainty, on just about everything. Exactly where the enemy was and what combat would be like once engaged. The sounds may be the worst of the experience. With all the smoke bombs going off, which Brand's team used as an edge, their sight was gone, but the sounds of screaming and crying were rampant. They would frighten harden soldiers, which most of the defenders were not.

There are two natural instincts: to follow the sound and fight, or to avoid them. Brand was leading the group, making him the point man. Others tried to reason with him, but after watching for so long, he wanted combat.

They were in a tank formation with the Brothers on either side of Jayne and Brand in front of them, the rest behind Jayne, and the Brothers spread out, forming a triangle.

Brand's weapon was very effective against The First People. Without the time crystal, it would not last long using that type of power that his lasers had. That is also what powered his energy shield, allowing it to take multiple hits with no ill effects to the wearer.

He would take many blasts that would kill most by de-powering their body shields and then destroy the occupant inside it. His weapon reach was longer than their swords, and since it seemed like he could take unlimited blasts, he killed many.

Brand was moving towards his left, heading into the bamboo field. That area was less flat than the main battlefield. As they moved, unbeknownst to them, The First People's command moved soldiers to that area. They were able to track Brand via the chip inside his head.

To them, that was not cheating, as the chip itself gave Brand many advantages. It was considered an even exchange, making it fair for both sides to use.

At one point, there were three First People killing five warriors and two field aids providing food, medicine, and ammunition. Brand became enraged, charging at the three invaders. Between himself and his group, only two of his personal warriors died, while all three First People fell at that moment.

Brand's group had shrunk to under 20 when they finally hit the bamboo field. Brand had laid down to sleep, which even with all the sounds the body will take over and pass out.

A field aid called Cake came to the group. She was young and had reloaded them with food and ammunition for the troops. Manny was talking with her when he mentioned Plutoneus' name and said that he was sleeping.

Cake was astonished that their great leader was fighting right here with them when Manny replied.

"Cake, trust me, Plutoneus is honored that you are fighting here with us, helping us. Do you want me to wake him so you can meet him, and he can personally tell you the same?"

Now Cake, who was blushing, said, "No, please let our great leader rest. Just being around him and knowing he is here with us means so much!"

With that, she moved on. What a brave soul. She had been on the field for over three days, and many did not last hours.

The rest of the volunteers had entered the field, and it was only the fourth day of fighting. Not only were they losing badly, but also were the other races that had joined the fight on their side.

These First People loved war and battle. Most were smiling as they killed without a care. It was not just their size or zeal for destroying the enemy. It was their attitude. They were enjoying themselves and having fun, which made everything happening feel worse.

Many areas now had no smoke covering their scenes of death. More than just Brand now had dead stares. They would rummage the dead for valuables such as food, power packs, ammunition, or weapons.

They had finally made it to the bamboo field, yet the time it had taken erased any advantage it may have provided.

Brand's group was now stuck in a half-circular valley, which they were located at the bottom of. That area was lower than the rest of the valley. It was a bad position, and now they had been boxed in. The longer they were there, the more assuring of their doom.

Manny was conferring with Brand, Dabs, and the Brothers. Of course, Jayne was next to Brand. Manny wanted to try to slip out one of the sides with the Brothers leading the charge. It became a heated argument, hearing the following from Brand.

"I will lead the charge. Once it is cleared, the rest can follow."

"That is just crazy, Boss. Please let's all rest for the charge ahead, okay?"

"Okay!" Was the answer, more a shout of defiance.

The group of 20 were getting as comfortable as could happen when you are hurt, hungry, and know death is near. Eating some rations that Cake had provided, a few were actually smiling. War was so strange like that, certain death and yet just another day in the battle of life.

As they were resting, relaxing, all of a sudden, shouting came from one of the Brothers.

"He is on the move! He is moving! Come on, we must go!"

Brand had waited until everyone was relaxed and then started to run over the hill like he was on fire. He screamed curses as he went over the top, this was not a sneak attack.

His weapon had a longer reach than the enemy in front of him. His adrenaline plus dopamine were flooding his system. Even with his yelling, he still had taken them by surprise.

Brand's weapons were shooting even longer than usual, with a greater spread than before. It appeared they were connected to his body's chemistry and gaining extra power from it. The chip in his head could do amazing things.

As he killed many First People, he was taking so many body energy shots that it looked as if he were blinking like a spotlight that was faulty, staying on target but not able to keep illuminating its subject.

Brand had killed over 15 First People and was walking right into their fire, like a madman slashing so quickly from left to right, killing many before him.

His body shield finally just broke. The power source, its time crystal, was fine, but the suit just could not take that kind of continuous damage. It literally fell apart after a bunch of hissing sounds.

If Jayne had not been there, Brand would have surely died. She jumped in front of him, taking the next wave of blasts. A moment later, one of the Brothers pulled Brand down and moved him to the side, gaining safety. They had gotten out and could now move freely in the bamboo field again.

Jayne had to be left there with all the dead bodies. Brand had lost three more, not counting Jayne. They were moving back to the main battlefield. There were so many less walking while the dead now outnumbered the living.

This being the fifth day of fighting, those still walking around had stood the test of time in that regard. All now being battle-weathered fighters that, through luck, brains, and courage, had survived this long.

26

TEARS

Bubba could not stop watching while feeling the pain of the defenders below. He was not worried about when they would lose, what would happen to him and Dragonfly. No, it was just sadness for the scene below.

Dragonfly had been working on something for hours. Actually, she had been working on it since she heard the call to defend the galaxy.

Rarely did Bubba interrupt her, but he could not take any more of the scene he was watching. He knocked on her door. She responded that she would be right out. He could tell she was being very secretive about whatever role she had to play regarding the conflict unfolding below.

Once she left the room, the door closed behind her, and she looked at Bubba.

"Captain Jones, I assume it is going very badly down there, and you want to know if I am going to help."

Bubba was just looking at her. She was so brilliant in her mental abilities. It was like being with Sherlock Holmes.

Dragonfly continued, "All is now ready for my meeting with The First People-"

Bubba now interrupted, "You're not going to meet them. It's too dangerous."

Dragonfly was touched by his concern, "You are right. I am setting up a virtual meeting where they will not be able to harm either of us in any way."

She continued, "I have sent them a request and expect them to respond shortly!"

Now Bubba was more curious than before, which was a lot. He asked, "How can you be certain that they will respond, let alone in a positive way?"

Looking at her Captain, she gave him a wink as she answered.

"Because I am Dragonfly!"

Now, that was half the real reason, with the remaining being it had to be answered.

The pace on the battlefield had changed. At first, there was an urgent need to engage in combat quickly, especially because of the way The First People were fighting. Now, there was a much slower speed to things.

Even with more reinforcements entering the fields, mostly from other species than Earth-type beings, The First People had not added much more than what they had started with.

Truth had to be given that no one in this galaxy had ever witnessed greater fighters than what was before them. You could tell as vicious as they were, they had their own code to war.

It felt like now the few that were left would be killed with more dignity than the others. Given they had survived this long.

The general feeling was that it would be over by tomorrow, if not by the end of this day. They had given them their best shot, but it was not even close to enough.

Brand's group had merged with other defenders, bringing their numbers to about 300 people. Some were currently resting while others were guarding the position. Brand still had Manny, Dabs, and the Brothers, plus a few more of his original team. All the others were gone.

There were piles and piles of bodies. Making artificial walls on the field to be navigated by all who were left.

As he was sitting, it hit him, and that was when his tears started to streak down his face. It was so unfair and unjust that he should still live while someone like Jayne was now gone. Making it so much worse that she died to save him. A debt that can never be repaid, a weight to carry for life. The guilt grew inside while the tears flowed on the outside.

One of the Brothers had seen it and contacted Manny about what should be done.

Manny approached Brand, "What's your orders, boss?" Manny had so many talents, knowing that currently, Brand needed to refocus on the living.

Brand wiped his cheeks with his hand, which left dirty streaks that had been created by his tears and dirt.

"Get as many warriors together as you can, I want to tell you all something."

"Yes, boss."

————

Virtual meeting rooms were standard within the galaxy. It provided all occupants safety plus a more personal experience. Dragonfly had sent a request for an audience, which had now been accepted.

She was seated on a throne, dressed in elegant silk dress with a red and black floral print that had a Japanese style. Wearing beautiful jewelry and having her hair done in a special way, she was ready to make her appearance.

They appeared in her room, also sitting on elaborate wooden chairs with fine fabrics covering the seats and armrests. Finely carved details were etched into the wood.

There were three First People sitting across from Dragonfly, she was outnumbered, yet it seemed balanced, and fair given her capabilities.

"Thank you for granting my request. I am called Dragonfly and wish to speak on the terms of your withdrawal from this galaxy. I do not make threats, so take my words seriously or face your peril."

Only one person spoke in the exchange, being the one sitting in the middle of the three First People who faced her.

"We know who you are and what you are capable of creating. There are things that cannot be thought nor spoken. We believe you know of these things. We will leave this galaxy and not return on one condition. We will take Brand Wright and whoever is around him. That is not negotiable! Do you accept?"

It was amazing that they both knew what the other was referring to without ever having to mention it. A true sign of each's brilliance, Dragonfly was truly their equal, and they acknowledged that fact. Even with the ultimate destruction of everything, without taking Brand, there would be no deal.

Dragonfly said, without hesitation, "Agreed."

To The First People, this was not a defeat. They came for Brand, and there are 200 billion galaxies in the universe. They would have plenty to conquer, and when Dragonfly died of natural causes, they will come back to take this one.

27

LAST CHARGE

The sky had a pinkish-grey tone, and the weather felt more relaxed than it had been. There were less than 400 around Brand, mostly warriors but also some field aids. Brand had been talking with Dabs and the Brothers, giving instructions regarding some future action.

Brand called Manny over, wanting to go over some plans before he spoke to the group. The First People had now brought four more huge ships into existence on Brand's side of the field. They had eight ships forming a circle around the main field that Brand and his group were located on.

Their soldiers had moved to the side of the field, forming a circle around the defenders. Most had re-entered their crafts as if they were preparing something inside.

Dabs was standing next to Brand with Manny, a few feet in front of them both. The Brothers, who were always around, were now on either side of Manny.

Brand, looking at Manny, commanded, "I want you to go past the command center to the safe zone."

Manny, who always supported Brand, looked hurt. It seemed like any other order would be fine, but not that one.

Manny asked with a bit of anger, "Why, what do you want me to do?"

"Live." Was Brand's answer.

Then, he looked at Dabs like *told you, now do it.* Dabs, who had his gun out, which was not unusual given where they were, shot one blast that was just strong enough to knock Manny out without any long-term consequences.

Before his knees touched the ground, the Brothers had supported him, placing each of his arms around their necks.

Brand now said to them, "Go," and then looking at Dabs, "You go too. They will let you leave the circle."

The Brothers said, okay, but that they would be returning.

Dabs looked at Brand with defiance, "No, can't do that."

Brand knew he would not change his mind. Like Jayne, Dabs was committed to more than just staying alive. His love for his girl, which, whenever mentioned, brought a wonderful smile to his face, was his promise. He would not break that even in death's sight.

Like so many who had died and so few who were now left on this field, their love for others was greater than life itself.

Brand, still looking at Dabs, asked, "Dabs, you're always talking about your woman. What's her name?"

"Italya. She is so beautiful, funny, wonderful, and sexy..." Dabs just kept going on, which to the people around him was nice. Brand could see in their faces that each had their own Italya.

Brand looked like he was trying to get something to work inside his head, as his eyes seemed to be focusing on something no one else could see.

Even though the Brothers were strong, they were tired, and Manny was not light, being completely immobile. As they approached their side of the field, there were First People that had surrounded the entire area, closing off the entrance they needed to get to.

The two Brothers looked at The First People, making eye contact while still holding up Manny. It lasted a few seconds before they moved away from either side of the entrance to the command center.

There was mutual respect for each other, the winners and losers. They were great fighters, staying outnumbered when they easily could have added more soldiers. Their skill and bravery in killing had to be appreciated.

On the other side, these two had lasted all they had given and were still standing. More than that, helping an injured man to safety, they deserved the path they were on.

To many, it may be crazy. Just hours ago, they were fighting with the joy of killing each other and now honor given to all who were left.

They moved Manny first to the command center, figuring he would be safe. They wanted to get back to what now felt like home, the killing fields. That was how, by the second day, they were referred to by many.

Their orders were to the safe zone, which was another two miles past their current location. What seemed long was really only a couple of minutes. After soul searching, for they really wanted to leave Manny at the command center, they did what they were told. They left Manny with people who were still waiting there and started their way back from the safe zone as quickly as they could.

Brand had been able to take over the loudspeakers that were located in different areas of the field. Not only were The First People amazing fighters, but they had also created some of the most advanced technology the galaxy had ever seen. The chip continued to be able to do so much more than translation.

With the proper thoughts given in his mind, the chip somehow figured out a way to make it happen.

Looking over the rag-tag group before him, they had suffered much by answering the call and now were closer to their death than ever before.

Brand's back became straighter, and energy flowed from his voice as if a great second wind had entered his body.

"We have won the battle! Saved the day! We have shown them who we are and how tough we are! I am proud of each being here, honored to have you by my side! Hold your heads high. I know it may not feel it, but we have won!"

Then Brand looked at the other side, the invaders' side, shouting the following.

"Is that all you got?! We have not even started to fight!"

Then quietly, almost talking to himself, "This is for Jayne."

Brand started to run towards The First People's side of the field. Beginning slowly and picking up mass, all the defenders followed him. They were yelling and firing their weapons in the air as they ran across the field.

————

Bolt had Adam released from holding for the Final Battle, which was already taking place. He made it seem like he had tried to get him out sooner, yet he had been unable to do so until now.

They were watching when Adam asked, "Why is he doing that? It is obvious they have lost."

Bolt explained, "It is called the last charge. Rather than wait for death to come, you attack your enemy, showing they have not conquered your spirit. That dying means much less than living under their rule."

Bolt's thoughts were on Subject 9, for that was how his mind always referred to him. This is exactly how he wanted to go, knowing he would miss him for the rest of his days.

Adam had changed since they had first met. There was a coldness that resided where his lucky go-easy used to live. Even his face appeared to look different. The loss of Jayne and his inability to join the war changed him.

Nicholas Bolt thought, *some changes are permanent, not just the physical scars but how the mind forever sees things. Many times, it happens when people return from wars, but it can also be life and death situations. Between what they have done, they didn't do and especially have seen, they are forever permanently different. Adam had joined that group.*

King Utago was watching with over 25 people in his room, but no one said a word. It was plain to see the pain on their King's face. Utago had his right hand holding his forehead while his left hand was in a tight fist. It was not known whether he was more in pain by what he was seeing or the fact that he was not with the defenders.

To all the viewers watching the event, it was hard to watch and impossible to stop watching. The galactic feed broadcast was really good for Earth's standards. They had long past the 8K sharpness with holographic displays showing every detail in 3D.

Spotlights began to emanate from the ships around the circle. Each ship had its own light broadcasting its circle. They seem to have a frequency or vibration singular to each ship. Then, the lights started to move inwards, all merging together and forming one big circle on the battlefield.

It had a green color, which enveloped everything around it. As the circles collided together, their vibrations started to blend into one frequency.

Brand's warriors' movement, as they were running toward the other side, was decelerating, making it look like they were in slow motion.

Now, people who were not in the circle were running towards it. These were very brave souls. Cake and the Brothers were amongst that group, trying to get into the green circle. It now had formed green walls, creating a half dome over the area below it. Cake was coming from the left and was a bit closer to it than the Brothers, who were south of the dome.

One of the Brothers was 2 feet ahead of the other and beat Cake in entering the field of green.

As Cake went through and before the other Brother made it to that area, everything disappeared. Unfortunately for Cake, only half of her had actually entered the light before this occurred. She was dead, and the other Brother, who had not made it there, was alive.

Everyone else in the field was gone, not just the people but the ground below them as well. There was an 8-foot drop to a flat surface devoid of all things.

It happened like a light switch, just a blink and the ground, the people, were never there. The First People were now getting into their ships surrounding the field. One by one, they blink off, leaving no sound or sight that they ever had been there.

In the aftermath of their visit, the area not affected by the light was surrounded by bodies, so many bodies.

28

GOOD AND SAD EFFECTS

Dragonfly had started an anonymous rumor of what happened, with the point being that The First People would not be back. She made sure it could not be traced back to her and that it reached the right ears.

It was over, yet things were different now. There had been a change in the galaxy's emotional well-being. It started slowly; its presence kept growing.

Things not only repeat themselves, but they form different versions, from the singular experience to a group mentality.

Imagine when a person meets a life-and-death experience. For some, it will change them forever. They realize how precious life is, how quickly it can disappear, and what is really important.

That experience can change how they think and respond to all the things that happened after that event. Now, all with different actions that are coming from the new enlightenment.

That process started in the galaxy. The core decided that profit was not the way to longevity, science and technology would be the answer. Also, people's happiness within the galaxy was important in maintaining the galaxy's strength in fighting off other enemies and creating a more harmonious mood, which had other positive benefits.

Working together, they would be stronger, providing greater security. This philosophy stopped wars that had been going on for centuries between planets. It was profound in its effect in changing so much for so many people.

The planet Fattalla became a holy place, the missing field, holy ground. No one was allowed to ever touch it. They had built a walkway around the hole, which was visited by billions. There was nothing for them to see but the hole, yet they came with many tears.

There were statues, plaques, and many other visual and written forms to honor all those who perished. They were well documented before the battle, which was greatly appreciated now by those who were left.

Even with all the benefits of the war, the survivors were so damaged.

All who did not die were heroes, period. They were the hardest hit from the battle. Manny, who always supported Brand, never asked for any special treatment and fought by his side through it all, was alive while the rest were gone. He was angry that Brand made that happen. He was loyal and dedicated, never asking to survive, now a refugee from the killing fields.

He became an unwanted celebrity and celebrated wherever he went. The questions never stopped: What was it like? What was Plutoneus really like? Eventually, he isolated himself from everyone except his family and very close friends, never being able to go out in public without the questions and pictures.

His thoughts were what happened to his friends. How he really wished he was with them, regardless of wherever that was.

If Manny's story was sad, the other Brother that was left could only be described as a tragedy. They were together their entire lives, choosing to just call themselves the Brothers. They were two but acted as one, working in unison. Combined with their size and intelligence, they were incredible.

Never actually being too far apart physically. If you saw one, you would see the other. He also became a hero and a star celebrity, yet he would give it all up in a second to be back with his brother. To understand his type of suffering, that type of survivor's guilt, is almost impossible for most of us.

Cake became a symbol of what the galaxy needed to become. Because of her infectious spirit and the documentation done before the battle, she emerged as a great hero in the struggle for the galaxy's survival. Her image appeared on many planets in statues and pictures of all that is good. She became the face of true devotion for others' benefit.

Jayne Stillwater also received a special place in all stories. Her bravery in all she did to get there and then save Plutoneus from certain death was honored throughout the galaxy.

As for Brand Wright being in the Final Battle, that never happened. On Earth, Plutoneus was mentioned, but there was never a connection to Brand. Bubba Jones and Jayne Stillwater were named, receiving their well-earned accolades. Bubba was always referred to as Captain Jones.

Another glaring omission not just on Earth but throughout the galaxy was Dragonfly's name, which was never mentioned.

Nicholas Bolt, who now had Sam's job, had changed his thoughts regarding being around RBs. He enjoyed Adam company yet felt bad seeing the changes in him. Some were very positive, and others were needed for his new assignments, but still, he felt they were creating another Subject 9.

Adam asked why Brand was never mentioned, especially because of his extensive role in the whole affair.

Before Bolt could respond, Adam said the following.

"You know the story going around is not true. What really happened?"

Bolt answered with a question, "Do your special abilities tell you anything about the truth on that day?"

Adam, now looking annoyed, "Why would I ask if I knew."

Bolt answered, "I truly don't know, but I agree with you. The story is more a fairy tale than what would make logical sense."

The irony is that so few really knew, and one person had a good suspicion. Even without knowing the truth, so many positive things occurred. Maybe if they had known the truth, none of that would have happened.

The story that was going around the galaxy, was that they answered the challenge of The First People. With such bravery and strength, that after five days, they acknowledged our superiority and left, never to return to this galaxy.

There were many holes if investigated, but most were quick to accept that version. Of course, there were conspiracies of all different thoughts. Why would The First People leave when they killed almost all who showed up to fight them? They obviously were better fighters and had incredible technologies. It made no sense.

To most of the public, it was much easier to believe the made-up scenario since the attack was over and the invaders were now gone. Why dig too deep? The problem was resolved, and that was all that mattered.

29

THOUGHTS

It has been said that the pen is mightier than the sword, yet there is something that is greater than the word written by that pen.

Before the word becomes a word, there is a thought. The power in thoughts is the beginning of all things. Once the thought has created something out of nothing, it can then be expressed in words.

Take the atomic bomb. First, an idea in thoughts is converted to words from the thoughts. Yet once others know it is real, they will figure out how to create this thought on their own. The original thought, after becoming a reality, will be done by others who never had the original thought.

This is why the galaxy can never know the truth: that The First People, even with ultimate annihilation, would still not relinquish until they had what they came for.

All things follow a pattern that resembles each other. In the simplest terms, they are born, grow, and die. Between growth and death, it can last over a long period of time, being part of a natural cycle, or be suddenly terminated.

Whether it is a human being, planet, sun, galaxy, or universe, all have a natural and unnatural ending. Once it is understood that just the thought of how the universe could be destroyed in the right minds would lead exactly to that.

It would start small but continuously get larger, being self-feeding in its destruction.

Bubba was having breakfast with Dragonfly when he started with his thoughts.

"Nothing adds up. The story going around just doesn't make any sense. And with all the news about everyone who was involved, there is not a word about you."

Dragonfly had been happier lately, and it had shown not just in her personality but also in her looks. She appeared younger now than when they first met."

"Captain Jones, I like being anonymous and am quite pleased not to be known in that affair." Hoping that would be enough to quench his thirst for knowledge, she tried to move on with their plans for the day.

"Are you ready to visit the most wonderful planet in the Perseus arm of our galaxy? They are aware of our visit, and I have reservations for one of their finest views."

Bubba stayed on the prior subject and continued.

"I know you did something to make them leave and not come back. The whole galaxy should be thanking you! What really happened? Why did they leave?"

That was one of the many things she loved about Captain Jones. His intelligence was surprisingly good. He had a knack for knowing the truth and untruth when he encountered it. She would never tell him or anyone else what really happened. That she was ready to end the universe if they did not leave or if they came back. It was that close between everyone surviving and total destruction for all everywhere.

She hugged him and whispered in his ear, "Captain Jones, you are so wise, and you know we have no secrets, but this one thing can, never be told!"

The end.

EPILOGUE

If information is the valued commodity of the Universe, then secrets are their bank accounts. Nicholas Bolt had many secrets, one which led his interest into the Reality Bender's program.

From an early age he had clairvoyance that were very accurate. He kept tracked of them, which lead him to find others that had unique abilities, usually associated with the paranormal.

This aspect of his life was a strong influence which eventually led him to be the director of the Reality Bender's program.

His thought went to how he tried to warn Sam Smith about Pierce, with no success coming from it. He wondered what they would do if they knew he also had reality bender capabilities.

Bolt had watched the battle closely and reviewed certain scenes when he realized what was missing, that there was a chance.

Nicholas Bolt had a more hands on approach than Sam, his predecessor. He had a starship take him to Fattalla. They did not land but were in orbit, he had a hunch and, if right, wanted to be close to the point of contact.

The captain contacted him saying he had a call waiting for him. The private study off the bridge was available if he wanted to use it.

Bolt maneuvered his way to the bridge and then study. It was not a phone but a headset he used. The agent on the other end began.

"Sir, we did find her, and she is alive! she was incredibly lucky and very close to death, but her recuperative powers are very strong. We all will be back onboard in two hours. Is there anything else you want done?"

Nicholas Bolt let a smile slip onto his face and replied, "Not currently. Well done."

He opened his computer to a program he knew very well, created a new folder, and titled it: Subject 128 - Jayne Stillwater.

Covers created by Brittany Wilson

May 9, 2024

Well my friends, if you are reading this page then I will take it as you still want more. Here I must acknowledge certain people that have played a part in this book's creation.

First without my readers, yes you, who are reading this, none of this matters! It is my sincere hope that you have enjoyed this book and feel that you got your money's worth. Thank you for your support!

Brittany Wilson created this wonderful front, spine and back covers. She is wonderful to work with, and her talents are reflected in the finished products. She can be contacted at https://www.brittwilsonart.com.

Jason Shprintz, my son was the editor of this and all my books. His help with plot development in conjunction with his editing abilities always produces a much better final product. Thank you Jason for your honest review and all that you do!

Also Jason was the first author in the family. His book, THE REVERIE, inspired me to start writing. That and one other person, who will be left unmentioned.

This book is very special to me and I have tried to make each process the best it can be, better than all that came before it.

Writing is not a group sport, it is lonely, hard, yet the reward when people tell you how much they enjoyed your books, cannot be written into words. Like Brand on the battlefield telling his warriors they will be remembered, I want to thank each reader and hope you know how much it means to me, that you have taken the time and expense to support my work.

I hope it has brought you smiles, tears, made you mad and given you a laugh for that was my intentions.

If you want to contact me please send your emails to bshprintz@mac.com.

Thank you!